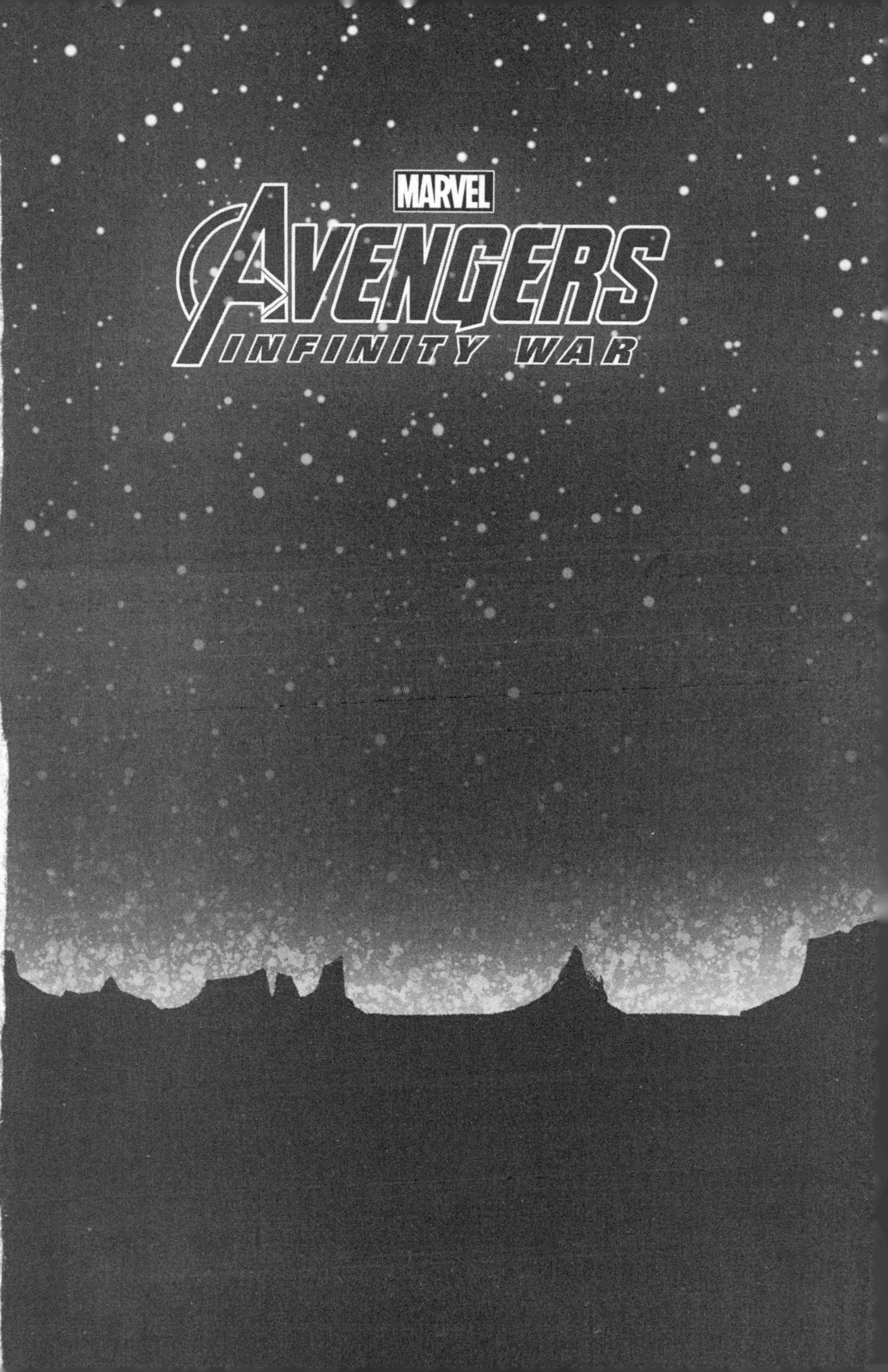
MARVEL
AVENGERS
INFINITY WAR

MARVEL

AVENGERS
INFINITY WAR

THE
COSMIC QUEST
VOLUME TWO: AFTERMATH

BRANDON T. SNIDER

LITTLE, BROWN AND COMPANY
New York   Boston

marvelkids.com

© 2018 MARVEL

Cover design by Ching N. Chan. Cover illustration by Matt Taylor.

Little, Brown and Company
Hachette Book Group
1290 Avenue of the Americas, New York, NY 10104
Visit us at LBYR.com

First Edition: November 2018

Little, Brown and Company is a division of Hachette Book Group, Inc. The Little, Brown name and logo are trademarks of Hachette Book Group, Inc.

The publisher is not responsible for websites (or their content) that are not owned by the publisher.

ISBNs: 978-0-316-48287-5 (paper over board), 978-0-316-48279-0 (ebook)

Printed in the United States of America

LSC-C

10 9 8 7 6 5 4 3 2 1

CONTENTS

PROLOGUE

Millions of people across the globe faded from existence without a trace. Their bodies turned to ash and scattered into the wind. There was no warning, no preparation, and no explanation. The world was left without answers. As humanity struggled to make sense of its new normal, a passionate scientist named Erik Selvig believed the event pointed to something much bigger. He slowly began assembling the puzzle pieces to determine what.

Once the head of Theoretical Astrophysics at Culver University, Selvig had been an admired figure in the scientific community for decades. His life's work suddenly changed the day Thor Odinson appeared on Earth. This fantastic encounter forced Selvig to reconsider everything he thought he knew about the nature of the universe. Earth was now one small part of a grand cosmic tapestry. Selvig's resources expanded, his ideas became bolder, and his work fulfilled him more than ever. Sadly, it wouldn't last. Thor's brother, Loki, used a powerful Scepter to control Selvig's mind and abuse his intellect for evil purposes. Innocent lives were lost, and Selvig was left devastated and confused. The experience had shattered him. The healing process was difficult and time-consuming. Slowly but surely, his mental prowess returned. But with Earth's population decimated, Selvig struggled to maintain his sanity in a world without answers.

CHAPTER 1

"Erik, are you in there? And if so can you just...
open up...please?"

Darcy Lewis had been knocking on the door of Room 212 at the Seafarer Motor Inn for the past fifteen minutes. Much to her frustration, Selvig wasn't answering. She wasn't 100 percent positive he was even inside, but it was where he'd *said* he'd be. Selvig called her in the middle of the night, demanding she join him on an unspecified quest. Normally, she'd tell him to relax, that they'd talk about it in the morning. By then he would've moved on to some other pressing scientific matter. This time was different. He didn't sound like himself. His words were garbled. His voice trembled. It seemed as if he'd reached a breaking point. Being

3

the dutiful companion that she was, Darcy got in her car and drove. That kind of dedication wasn't in her official job description, but, then again, that description had changed quite a bit from the day she was first hired. The trip to New Mexico had been long and boring. Her radio didn't work, leaving Darcy with only her thoughts to keep her company. She feared the worst and hoped for the best. It took her all night, but she'd finally made it. There was no way she was leaving without answers.

"*Open the door, dude.* I'm seriously dying out here!"

Silence.

"I'm going to give you one minute to open this door, Erik. I don't know what exactly I'm going to do if you *don't* open this door, but I'm going to do *something*, and, trust me, you're not going to like it."

Darcy wiped the sweat from her brow and tried a different tactic.

"What if I told you I've got gummy worms, *hmm?* Would you open the door *then?*" Her voice took on a playful, singsongy tone. "They're *organic.*"

Darcy had never wanted to be an astrophysicist.

She hadn't even wanted to be a scientist. Not that she was, either. At best, Darcy was Erik Selvig's assistant. At worst? She didn't think about it. Her job began as a goof. Years earlier, she'd applied as a long shot to a summer internship. The next thing she knew, she was working for Selvig and Doctor Jane Foster, learning how to make a good cup of coffee and dodge entities from other dimensions. Suddenly, her political science classes didn't seem as interesting. At first, she was insecure about her role. She didn't have the scientific background, but she was smart and quick on her feet. That's all that mattered to Selvig. The job took her all over the world, but the long hours kept her from family and friends. Birthday party? Darcy had to work. Vacation? Darcy had to work. Though she never showed it, she started enjoying the job less and less. Selvig's erratic behavior put a strain on things. She did her best to support him, but he'd become difficult to deal with. Darcy wondered if it was time to move on.

"Ugh. Whatever, dude. I give up." As she turned to walk away, Darcy heard a faint rustling inside the motel room. She rushed over to check. "Listen, Erik, it's time to get serious. I want you to listen *very carefully*, okay? When you open that door, I swear to God, Odin, and whoever else is up there—*you'd better have clothes on*. I'm talking one hundred percent covered. Not a *hint* of anything. A girl's gotta put her foot down. Run around in your undies as much as you want on your own time, but *I'm* here now. There will be *zero* nakedness. Put on some pants and open up! It's hot as you-know-what out here." She cupped her hands around her ear and tried to hear through the door. Despite the tease of progress, she was met with nothing but silence. "I bet Pepper Potts never has to deal with stuff like this."

Darcy strolled over to the rusty metal railing that overlooked the motel grounds. The place was teeming with curious characters. Poolside, a woman clipped her toenails and flicked them into the water while her husband lathered himself in cheap tanning oil. A mangy dog, possibly blind, wandered, while bumping into things and barking angrily at nothing in particular. Two twin boys, covered in dirt, played peekaboo in a mud puddle near the edge of the parking lot. Their mother and father argued over who'd clean them up. The motel's owner, Ken, did one-armed push-ups in the middle of the courtyard, looking around in between reps to see if anyone was watching. Darcy noticed a boy lingering near her in the open-air hallway, inching closer and closer. He seemed to be around twelve years old, dressed in a gray polo shirt and jeans, with a head full of tight black cornrows. She saw that he was smiling, but she couldn't figure out why. "Can I help you with something?" she asked.

"Doctor Selvig is probably sleeping," he said. "He stays up all night, sleeps all day. It's his routine. He thinks he's not predictable, but he totally is. I know his patterns."

"Thanks for the heads-up," Darcy replied.

"Do you believe in supernatural forces?" the boy asked. "Only an idiot wouldn't believe in supernatural forces." He looked her up and down. "Not that *you're* an idiot."

Darcy was thrown for a loop. She remained

silent, hoping the kid would take the hint and walk away. No such luck.

"There are all these unexplained phenomena on our planet. Stuff we don't understand and will never understand. But there has to be a scientific explanation for everything. That's just how the universe works," he explained. "You agree, right?"

"Who *are* you, dude?" asked Darcy.

"Sorry. I'm Felix," he said, extending his hand for a shake. "You're Darcy Lewis. Doctor Selvig's assistant, right?"

Darcy shook Felix's hand. "I'm his *associate*, not his assistant, and *this* is a no-tween zone. That means no tweens within this zone," she said, swirling her fingers in a circle.

"Has he told you his theory yet?" Felix asked. "Doctor Selvig knows the truth behind what happened. Or at least he thinks he does. I don't know. He won't tell me. I hear him talking to himself about it at night, but that doesn't count."

"You seem nice, kid," Darcy said. "But I'm dealing with a situation here."

"My parents are immigrants. From Ethiopia," Felix said awkwardly. "They moved here about twenty years ago, and I was born about eight years after that. They were scientists like Doctor Selvig. Biologists, actually."

"Cool," Darcy said. Her patience was wearing thin. She looked in the other direction, hoping Felix would take the hint and leave her be.

"They're, um, gone," Felix said softly. "Because of, you know...I'm on my own now." He shifted his eyes and shuffled his feet. "The therapist at my old school said that since I'm a prodigy, it's hard for me to communicate because I'm so smart. I have trouble relating to people because my mind goes, like, a million miles per hour. That's why Doctor Selvig and I get along so well, I guess."

"Erik's mind definitely goes a million miles per hour," Darcy said. "I'm really sorry to hear about your parents. Tough stuff, little man."

"Yeah." Felix looked out across the motel court-yard. Tears welled in his eyes. He wiped them away before they fell. "Sorry if it's weird that I brought them up like that. I can't help it. I miss 'em. The more I tell people about who they were and where they came from, the more it keeps their spirits alive. You know what I mean? Besides, the first law of thermodynamics, also known as the law of conservation of energy, states that energy can neither be created nor destroyed; only transferred or changed from one form to another. That means my parents, and everyone else we lost that day, are out there somewhere, just in a different form."

"That's a nice way of looking at things," Darcy said, smiling warmly.

Felix leaned closer to Darcy. "You wanna hear something freaky?" he asked. "Some of the relatives of the people who vanished at the Seafarer show up *every single day* just to see if their folks are back. The manager always calls the cops on them. He's a jerk like that." Felix stared at Darcy, unblinking. "You're way more basic-looking than I thought you'd be."

Darcy's expression turned sour.

"No shade. Most women your age are pretty basic overall. At least in my experience."

"In. Your. Experience?" she fumed.

FWOOSH!

A panic-stricken Erik Selvig swung open the door to his motel room. "Darcy!" he shouted. "What are you doing here?!" He craned his head down the hallway in both directions, checking to make sure she hadn't been followed. Selvig's gray hair was a wild mess. There was a fresh trail of drool that went from the corner of his mouth all the way down to his neck. He'd wrapped himself in bedding, covering his body in a cocoon-like toga.

"Don't *you* look *together?*" Darcy said, her eyes wide with sarcasm. "You called me last night, Erik. At three AM. You were going on about something I didn't understand, then the phone cut out. I tried calling you back, but it went straight to voice mail. I got in my car and drove here because I'm faithful to the cause. I'm also worried."

Selvig stared at her blankly.

"Do you remember *any* of this?"

Selvig remained silent.

"Hey, Doc," Felix said with a wave. "How's it going?"

"Felix," Selvig said with a kind nod. "My associate and I are conducting some very important business at the moment. Run along now."

Down in the courtyard, Ken, the manager, had just finished his exercise routine and was looking for a confrontation. "Felix!" he yelled. "Get down here and scrub these toilets! You wanna keep stayin' here, you gotta work. I ain't gon' tell you again."

Felix bolted. "Nice meeting you, Darcy. Talk to you later, Doctor Selvig!" he shouted, racing down the stairs to complete his task.

"What's his deal?" Darcy asked.

"Ken is a tyrant," Selvig groused. "*Always* in my business. I caught him cleaning my room the other day without my permission. And the rent? Highway robbery."

"I meant *Felix*."

"Oh. He's a very bright young man who has taken a shine to me," Selvig said. "He's in need of mentorship. Something I'm not in a place to provide at the moment."

"Clearly," Darcy said. Her clothes were damp

with sweat. "Are you going to invite me inside or what? I'm dying out here."

"Yes! Yes. Yes, come in," Selvig said, welcoming her into the room. He tossed away his covering to reveal a once-white XXL T-shirt, tattered around the edges and covered in powdered-cheese-crusted fingerprints.

Darcy entered the dark space, tripping gently over a pile of unwashed clothing. As her eyes adjusted, she realized that dirty clothes were just the beginning. "Holy…" She gasped, flipping on the light. Selvig's motel room was a total disaster. It was littered with trash and half-eaten food items. The smell was rancid, as if a mayonnaise-filled burrito had been stuffed in an old shoe, baked on high for a week, then simmered in liquid body odor. An enormous pile of sour towels sat in the corner of the room like a terry cloth snowman, melting in the heat. Darcy was confused by the trail of candy bar wrappers that went from the bed to the bathroom. The wallpaper had been torn down, replaced with Selvig's etchings of cubes, suns, wheels, trees, and other childlike formations. A crescent-shaped device had been drawn and crossed out. Sticky notes lined the perimeter of the room, each one filled with formulas and theories. The sight was overwhelming. Darcy didn't know where to begin. "Have you tried meditation?" she asked. "You should try meditation."

Selvig spotted the bag of gummy worms in Darcy's pocket and snatched it away. "Despite my disheveled quarters, I'm actually in a good place. The pieces of a great puzzle are coming together," he said, ripping open the bag and stuffing a handful of candy into his mouth. "This is where it all started for us, you know. The very first recorded sighting of an Einstein-Rosen bridge was right *here* in Puente Antiguo. That's why I came back. This location has significance. It has meaning. Remember when we first met? What a day *that* turned out to be, eh?"

"Do...you...need...a hug?" Darcy asked tentatively. "I'd give you one, but your clothes are filthy, and you smell like a pet store. Why don't we clean you up so we can go get some fresh air and a bite to eat, huh?"

Selvig reached under his bed, pulled out a crumpled bag of cheese twists, and poured them into his mouth. *"These* are very good," he crunched. "Let's eat these."

Darcy was done playing games. "What am I doing here, Erik?"

Selvig tossed away the cheese twists, grabbed the nearest two-liter bottle of soda, and chugged. After a lengthy burp, a sly smile crossed his face. "We're going to solve the riddles of the universe." Suddenly, his tone had changed. He was clearheaded and in control. "After the decimation event, my mental health stumbled. I was clouded, spewing out all manner of things. It's been a struggle to get back on track, but I can feel things changing for the better." Selvig paced through the room, looking for something he had trouble finding. "There was a time when humanity had no idea what lay beyond our world. As modern science evolved, we gazed deeper into the heavens. And what have we seen?" He paused for dramatic effect. *"Oh, what we have seen."* Selvig's eyes grew wilder. "The heavens gazed back at us. Earth became a cosmic focal point. From the first Einstein-Rosen bridge right here in New Mexico, to the unexpected decimation of humanity itself, the planet has attracted all manner of uncanny phenomena. Darcy, you and I have experienced both gods *and* monsters. Did you ever dream of such a thing?"

"In my youth, I *may* have written a diary entry about one day meeting a beautiful blond-haired guy with broad shoulders."

Selvig continued, undeterred. "Astronomers recently made a wonderful discovery in ghost particles. These tiny neutrinos arrived on our planet from deep space, yet we never feel them. They pass through our bodies, rarely interacting with their surroundings. Don't you see? It's possible that these ghost particles were somehow awakened by the chaotic energies Earth has been imbued with—an unavoidable by-product of the fantastic events that have occurred over the last few years. The Tesseract, the Aether, Loki's Scepter—these items of power have left behind a kind of cosmogonic toxicity, swirling through our atmosphere."

"Like cosmic backwash?" Darcy asked.

"Precisely!" Selvig exclaimed. "Humanity is *swimming* in cosmic backwash."

"Oh yeah. We're swimming in something all right."

Selvig snapped. "Why are you worried about the condition of this room when our universe is crying out to be heard?! Don't you care about *that*?!"

Darcy strode over to Selvig's desk. It was covered in drawings, formulas, and crumbs. She picked up a stack of papers and found what she needed. "Don't you care about *this*?" she asked, handing a photograph to Selvig.

"The three of us," he said. He grasped it tightly before flicking the photo onto the bed. Darcy calmly retrieved it, using her sleeve to give it a quick shine before placing the photo on the corner of a nearby mirror. "We need to find Jane."

"We've been through this before," Darcy explained. "Her phone is dead. Her emails bounce back. She probably went on an extended vacation."

"No, no, no. I reject this notion," Selvig said. "Jane and I have endured the same hardships. Our bodies have housed otherworldly forces. She and I should know the secrets of the universe, but they aren't"—he strained to find the right word—"clear. Not yet. But they will be. Jane will help us get to the bottom of this mystery. We'll figure out what caused this terrible tragedy, and we'll bring everyone back. *We'll bring them all back.*"

"We have to face facts, Erik. Jane might not be among the living anymore."

"Hogwash!" Selvig exclaimed. He paced back and forth through the minefield of trash. He reached under his bed, retrieved an empty bag of potato chips, and thrust his hand inside it. "And now I'm out of chips!"

Darcy took Selvig and moved his body in front of the mirror. "Get it together, Erik. Your pit stains have pit stains. Your hair is *crusty.* You need a shower, a shave, and a week's worth of sleep."

Looking at himself in the mirror, Selvig was overwhelmed with emotion. "I'm scared, Darcy." His lip quivered. "Humanity was decimated in the blink of an eye. The planet suffered an unimaginable loss.

My gut tells me the answers are out there, but I've never felt so afraid to find them. This is frighteningly new territory, and I'm ashamed to say I'm unprepared."

Darcy put her hand on Selvig's shoulder. "Take some time off. Get your head together. When you're feeling good again, we'll work it out. Sound good?"

"Now is the time for action!" a voice shouted from outside the room.

Darcy rushed to the door. She swung it open to find Felix wearing a fresh sport coat, a bow tie, and a joyous grin. "I was listening to your whole conversation and, um, hear me out—"

"Beat it," Darcy said. "I don't care how adorable you look right now. This is *not* the time." Darcy tried closing the door, but Felix pushed his way inside. "What do you think you're doing, dude?"

"Your job," Felix said, heading straight to Selvig. "Don't listen to her, Doc. *Now is the time.* You can fix everything. It's gotta be *you*," Felix pleaded. "You've been around a long time. You're, like, eighty years old, right?"

"I'm a fit sixty-five, thank you very much!"

"Really? You're only sixty-five?! Whatever. My point is, no one else has seen and experienced the things you have. The world needs answers and *she's* not going to find 'em," Felix said, pointing to Darcy. "There's only one guy on this planet who's suited to take on this mission, and its Doctor Erik Selvig. You're the GOAT, man!"

"There's no mission, *rude little boy*," Darcy said. "And, by the way, he doesn't know what *GOAT means*." She lunged to grab Felix and escort him from the room. He weaved to avoid her, laughing as he went.

"Ha-ha-ha-ha-ha! Someone's getting salty. Maybe that's because you're just jealous that *I've* got more scientific knowledge than you ever will...."

"Oh please! I'm not doing this with you, kid. What Erik needs is a vacation," Darcy pressed. "My great-aunt has a vacant condo in Florida. Fully furnished. Days at the pool, nights playing shuffleboard. The median age is sixty-five. Erik, you could get a girlfriend!"

Selvig scrambled around the room. "Felix is right. The time for action is *now*." He gathered his most important things and stuffed them into a backpack.

"Yes!" Felix exclaimed. "Now put on some pants. You're creeping everyone out."

Selvig quickly threw on a pair of trousers.

"The Tesseract, the Aether, the decimation event... it's all connected. Somehow. Doctor Jane Foster will be able to help us find those connections. She'll see the bigger picture. We must track her down at once." Selvig's tone was resolute. The decision had been made. He whipped off his T-shirt and replaced it with a crisp green Oxford. "That's better."

"Doctor Foster is one of my all-time heroes," Felix said. "I've been stanning her since back in the day."

Selvig's eyes narrowed. "What does that mean? *Stanning?*"

"It means I admire her," Felix said. *"A lot."*

Selvig smiled. "Then I'm *stanning* her as well!" He began furiously straightening the room. "There are a handful of, shall we say, *quirky* scientists I've shared ideas and theories with over the years.

Though we have fallen out of touch, these individuals may be able to help us in our quest."

"What quest?" Darcy bellowed. "I'm not dressed for a quest."

"Like I said. *Basic*," murmured Felix.

"In order to understand the decimation event, we must gather information from my old colleagues in person and without notice. The element of surprise! They'll be able to help us locate Jane. Once we've assembled our theories, we'll compare them all and make an educated deduction."

"Then?"

"We'll cross that bridge when we get to it!" Selvig cheered.

"Oh man, this is going to be *epic*," Felix said, straightening his bow tie. "Glad I'm camera ready, just in case."

Darcy threw up her hands. "Wait just a minute!" she shouted. "I haven't agreed to this yet. No one is going on a quest without *me*, okay? *I'm the one with the car.*"

Selvig stopped what he was doing. "You've always

followed me to the ends of the earth, Darcy. I'm forever grateful for your commitment. There are few people I trust completely. You're one of them. Please. Help me do what needs to be done to heal the planet."

"That's a broad request, but I like how you sprinkled in some very truthful compliments. Suppose I can't say *no* to that." Darcy almost smiled as Selvig wrapped his arms around her and squeezed. "But we're not taking the twelve-year-old."

"*I'm almost thirteen* and have a much higher IQ than you do," Felix said. "You're not leaving me at this dump. I'm probably days away from being snatched up by Child Protective Services. Then I'll end up in the foster-care system where who knows what'll happen." He shook his head and wagged his finger. "I'll never fulfill my potential—that would be a crime against humanity. Do you really want that on your conscience? I don't think you do, girl."

Selvig considered the proposal. "Welcome aboard, m'boy. Help me gather my things, would you?"

"Don't get in the way," Darcy said. The trio

collected a few of Selvig's personal items and headed out to the parking lot. "Ugh, this is all happening too fast! I really hope the *Mary Jackson* can handle this trek."

The name piqued Felix's interest. "Mary Jackson? The famous mathematician and aerospace engineer? What's she got to do with this?"

"Ta-da!" Darcy said, presenting her rusty red hatchback. The two-door vehicle was coated in soot and looked as if it could fall apart at any moment. "I named my car after her. She's my inspiration. The *Mary Jackson* may be a relic from the early nineties, but her spirit is timeless."

"This car is trash." Felix groaned. "The real Mary Jackson, however, remains a queen."

Ken spotted Felix, Darcy, and Selvig and hastily approached them. "Where do you think you're going, boy? The toilets are still dirty," he growled.

Felix took a long, deep breath. "Ken, thanks for giving me a job in exchange for a place to stay. That was kind. *However.* One act of kindness doesn't forgive the fact that you treat people like garbage and are, on the whole, a massive jerk. Take your toilet brush and—"

Darcy pushed Felix into the back seat and shut the door. "We're leaving now."

Felix rolled down the window and stuck his head out. "There will be no cleaning toilets today or ever again!" he shouted.

Ken strained to maintain his composure. "You owe me money, Selvig."

"A wire transfer is in progress, I assure you," Selvig replied. He shut the door as Darcy started the engine. "See you 'round. We're going to save the world."

"We'll see about that," grumbled Ken.

Darcy swung the *Mary Jackson* out of the parking lot and onto the road.

"So, Erik, where you wanna go?" Darcy asked.

CHAPTER 2

"Here. Here! *Here!*" Selvig screeched. "Darcy, turn HERE!"

Darcy's body tensed. *"Quit yelling,"* she snapped.

The six-hour road trip had been relatively uneventful. Felix and Darcy had argued until Selvig demanded silence for the remainder of the drive. Five hours and fifty-seven minutes later, they'd reached their destination: Lil' Odessa, Texas. The welcome sign read JUST LIKE ODESSA BUT LIL'.

The town's shopping district was once a bustling center of commerce—a nice respite for travelers on their way to somewhere more important. That was a long time ago. As years passed, almost all the once-prosperous businesses closed. Main Street was now littered with empty storefronts, such as Video Gulch, Illusia's Hair Salon, and Tank Top City, that were covered in graffiti. The only retail outlet that remained was the enigmatic Dollar Holler.

Felix poked his head into the front seat. "Seriously? Are there *any* people here, or did they all evaporate?"

"Pull over," Selvig said. Darcy swung into a parking spot and exhaled. Dollar Holler's floor-to-ceiling windows were covered in large, brightly colored fluorescent orange posters. Each one advertised incredible deals.

OFF-BRAND WONDERS! AVERAGE CONTRAPTIONS! DISCOUNT MILK! YOU'LL NEVER BELIEVE THE PRICES!

Darcy eyed the posters suspiciously. "*I'll never believe the prices?* Please. The place is called *Dollar Holler,*" she said, rolling up her window.

Selvig put on a pair of dark sunglasses with silver mirrored frames. "Follow my lead," he said. "And play it *cool.*" He threw open the car door and stuck his legs out to stretch.

"Wait a second," said Darcy. "What are we doing here, exactly?"

Selvig huffed, puffed, and shifted in his seat. "You need to *trust* me," he grumbled. "I know what I'm doing."

"I just drove six hours to a junk shop in a ghost town," Darcy countered. "You want me to *trust* you? Give me an explanation as to why we're *here*."

For a brief, shining moment, it seemed as if Selvig were ready to provide a response.

"I gotta pee," Felix interrupted.

Selvig launched out of the car, slamming the door behind him and marching up to the storefront.

"Thanks a lot," Darcy said, rolling her eyes. "I had him *right* where I wanted him."

"*I'm gonna pee my pants*," Felix pleaded. "I've been holding it for three hours."

Darcy pressed a button, power-locking the doors. "Wanna try for *four*?" She chuckled.

"Okay, laugh!" Felix cried. "See what happens next."

"Baby should've worn a diaper," Darcy said. She unlocked the doors and exited the car. Felix followed behind, doing his best to keep it together. Selvig was creeping around the building, craning his head above the lengthy posters to get a look inside.

"A clever masquerade," Selvig muttered, eyeing the sign marked OPEN. He rushed to the front door, threw it open, and dashed inside. "Aha!" he shouted. The poor woman at the cash register was startled and confused. "You think I don't know what's going on here, *but I do.*"

"May I help you, sir?" the woman asked, smile beaming. She was a tiny thing in a billowy pink blouse. Blonde curls erupted from her head and fell over her shoulder pads. Thin reading glasses, decorated with colorful rhinestones, hung around her neck by a chain.

Selvig eyed her name tag. "Perhaps you can enlighten me, *Zelda.* I'm looking for Alpha Tango 718."

"I'm sorry, hon. Is that motor oil?" Zelda leaned over the counter, glancing out across the store's numerous aisles. "Check next to the barrel of dream catchers, near the mayonnaise guns. We should have some in stock."

Selvig wasn't buying it. "You're very good," he said, pointing his finger in Zelda's direction. "She taught you very well, indeed."

Darcy stepped in to diffuse the situation. "Pardon me, ma'am, but he's going through a lot right now. You know how grandpas can be."

"She's lying. I'm childless," Selvig declared. "Childless!"

Darcy elbowed Selvig in his side. "He gets confused. *A lot.* What can I say? Mercury must be in retrograde," Darcy said with a confused shrug.

"I don't know what that means," declared Zelda.

"Me neither!" Darcy replied. "We'll try and stay out of your hair."

Felix had been waiting patiently to use the bathroom and was nearing his breaking point. Selvig motioned for him to come closer. "Felix, this may look like an ordinary bauble-filled shopping facility, but it's much more than that," he whispered, slinking down one of the aisles like the world's most obvious spy. "Keep watch for me."

"Your friend is on a mission, huh?" Zelda said. "What's he looking for again?"

"Oh, you know, *deals*." Darcy sighed. "You wouldn't happen to have a spare Tesseract around here, would you?"

"I'm afraid we don't stock Tezza-Rats," Zelda said. "Sorry 'bout that."

A variety of sharp aromas filled Darcy's nostrils. "Lots of potpourri in here, huh? I'm getting lavender, strawberry, and... bacon?"

"We have the second widest selection in the county," Zelda grinned.

"I need to *pee*!" Felix howled, desperately holding himself together.

"Oh, hon, bathrooms are for paying customers only," Zelda said, nodding toward the security camera in the corner. "Rules are rules, and I don't want to get in any trouble." Her eyes widened strangely as if she were being held hostage.

"They're *watching* us, eh?" Selvig said, poking his head out from behind a display.

Darcy reached into a nearby bin of trinkets and pulled out a heart-shaped key chain. "How much?" she asked, tossing it onto the counter. "I'll be the paying customer."

"One dollar," Zelda announced proudly.

Darcy handed Zelda a dollar bill as Felix raced away to take care of business. "Thank you!" he squealed, sprinting toward the bathroom.

"That's so sweet," Zelda said, placing Darcy's key chain in a small plastic bag. "I've got a son, too. I'd do *anything* if he needed to use the bathroom."

"Oh. Um. Gross?" Darcy mumbled. "Also—he's not my son."

"She's childless," Selvig shouted from the other side of the store. *"We're all childless!"*

"Pipe down, Grandpappy," Darcy yelled through gritted teeth. "Zelda, let's get real for a sec. What's up with this place?"

The bewildered look on Zelda's face indicated that she didn't understand the question.

"My grandpa seems to think your store isn't *just* a store," Darcy explained.

"He's right," Zelda chirped. "The Dollar Holler is a complete savings experience!"

Darcy pressed harder. "Are you *sure* you don't know him? Because we're on a mission to find some old friends of his, and he seems *convinced* this is a place we're supposed to be."

Felix exited the bathroom, relieved. "I can live again!" he declared.

Selvig marched up to the counter with a crumpled-up ten-dollar bill in his hand and tossed it in Zelda's face. She whipped her hand up, catching the bill with ease and precision.

"My turn," Selvig said, sauntering toward the bathroom.

Zelda's sweet demeanor shifted. She wasn't going to let Selvig out of her sight.

"Nice reflexes, Zel," Darcy complimented.

"I play softball," replied Zelda. "And I practice judo on the weekends." Her eyes followed Selvig. "Now that I think about it, he does look darn familiar."

"He's got one of those faces," said Darcy. "Sometimes you just want to smack him."

Felix jumped in. "Doctor Erik Selvig is one of the top astrophysicists on the planet. The dude worked for NASA and S.H.I.E.L.D. He knows the Avengers. Ask him about wormholes. I dare you."

A light bulb went on in Zelda's head. "Oh! Oh, oh, oh!" she exclaimed. "He's the smarty-pants who lost his marbles and ran around in the buff on TV! That clip of him at Stonehenge always makes me and my hubby laugh."

"We like to call him smarty-*no-pants*," Darcy said. She rummaged through the bin of key chains to pass the time.

"I'd love to get his autograph for my niece. She's a big fan of the Avengers, especially after everything that's happened. You know, some people think the Avengers were involved in that whole"—Zelda leaned in close as if to share a secret—"people turning to dust thing. Not *me*, though. I think they're heroes. That Scarlet Witch? Oh my goodness, I hope she's okay. My niece just thinks she's magical."

Darcy spied a key chain shaped like a test tube and snatched it out of the bin. "I don't believe in magic," she said.

"There's this other Super Hero. Insect Lady? Or, maybe, she's a type of spider person? Saw her on the news one time. Redhead. I can't remember her name. My niece is into her, too. There are so many Super Heroes these days I just can't keep up." Zelda shook her head in disbelief. "Black Widow! That's it. Do you know Black Widow?"

Darcy dangled the key chain on the end of her finger. "Depends. You got nine more of these little guys?"

Zelda reached under the counter, grabbed a box full of test tube key chains, and placed it in front of Darcy. "Will *this* do?"

Darcy looked over each shoulder as if she were about to reveal the deepest, darkest secret she'd ever heard. "Black Widow?" she whispered. "Is my best friend in the entire world."

Zelda gasped, clutching the place on her neck where refined women wore pearls. She couldn't believe her luck. Before she had a chance to ask a question, Felix did. "You ever hear of Hank Pym? He's a famous scientist like Doctor Selvig. You probably didn't know that."

"The name rings a bell, *thanks*," said Darcy. "What about him?"

"Pym created these things called Pym Particles that give people the ability to change their size and shape on a subatomic level. When you're teeny tiny, space and time are immaterial."

Zelda stared at Felix without blinking. "Fun," she said kindly.

"I was thinking about different realms during the car ride," Felix said. "How to access them and stuff. Darcy, what do you know about the Water of Sight?"

"Oh! Is that the fancy spa?" Zelda tittered.

"It's not a spa," Darcy said. "And, Felix, don't bring that up in front of Erik."

"Why? He said it's the key to everything," Felix explained.

Darcy became annoyed. "*When* did he say that?"

"Wouldn't *you* like to know," Felix said, raising an eyebrow.

"Drop it, Felix. I'm serious." Darcy placed ten test tube key chains on the counter. "I'll take these, please."

"Wonderful choice. Who are they for?" Zelda asked, stuffing the key chains into another bag.

"Don't know yet." Darcy shrugged. "I'll see where the day takes me."

Zelda's tone changed from cheerful to cautionary. "I don't know what brings you to Lil' Odessa, but I'd be careful if I were you," she warned. "There are secrets under this town. You don't need to be sniffin' around where—"

CRASH!

The sound of shattering glass came from the bathroom.

"Uh-oh," Felix said.

Zelda scurried around the counter and raced to the back of the store. She tried opening the bathroom door, but it was no use. Selvig had barricaded himself inside.

"I'm comin' in! Get ready, smarty-no-pants!" Zelda slammed her shoulder into the door, bursting through the blockage, to find a very unexpected scene. Selvig, in his infinite wisdom, had attempted to climb through a tiny window that led to the alleyway outside. He'd accidentally gotten himself stuck in the process. Zelda helped him down to safety. "You're a real piece o' work, you know that?" She pushed him down onto the floor, kneeing him in the back to keep him stationary.

"You don't understand. There's been a terrible mistake," Selvig pleaded.

"Zelda, those judo lessons are really paying off, sister. High five!" Darcy held up her hand, but Zelda wasn't interested.

"I want you out of my store," Zelda demanded. "I don't care if you're some famous scientist. You can't just come in here, break my windows, and do anything you want. Not here! Not in Zelda's house!"

She picked Selvig up, chucked him over her shoulder, and stomped to the store's entrance. "And to *think* I almost got your autograph for my niece." Zelda pushed open the door and tossed Selvig on his behind. Darcy and Felix shuffled out, deeply embarrassed by the bizarre episode that had just transpired.

"Sorry," Darcy said meekly.

Zelda shook her head with disappointment. She slammed the door shut and changed the sign in the window from OPEN to CLOSED.

Darcy plopped down on the curb next to Selvig. He was pouting. "Do you want to explain what happened in there?" she asked. "Or should we just get in the car and never talk about it again, because I would be totally cool with that."

"She was supposed to be here," Selvig said anxiously. *"She was supposed to be here."*

"Who?!" Darcy asked. "Who was supposed to be here? *You haven't told us.*"

Before Selvig had a chance to answer, a woman

poked her head out of a dilapidated storefront across the street. "Erik!" she shouted. "Over here!"

Selvig spotted her, and his frown immediately turned into a smile. "I had the wrong place," he said. "Simple mistake. Come, you two." He stood up and made his way across the street. "Everything is going to be just fine."

CHAPTER 3

"Anjelica!" Selvig exclaimed. "My dear, you are truly a sight for sore eyes." He rushed across the street, forgetting to look both ways. Thankfully, there wasn't any traffic in Lil' Odessa. Though he hadn't seen her in years, Selvig often thought about Anjelica Tan. They first met at the Scientific Frontiers conference. She was an astrobiologist who'd worked for NASA. Tan charmed Selvig with her humor and storytelling. They spent many late nights bonding over their shared love of the cosmos. They also loved to gossip. Tan claimed to know everything about everyone. Years later, Selvig hired Tan to work with him at S.H.I.E.L.D.'s Project P.E.G.A.S.U.S., where they studied the Tesseract day in and day out, and she grew to become one of his closest friends and colleagues.

After the incident with Loki, their working relationship ended, and their friendship suffered. As a result, they hadn't spoken or seen each other in a few years. Seeing her again filled Selvig with joy. She looked exactly as he remembered. Tan was a tall woman with soft features and a shaved head. She wore a sleek black suit. As Selvig moved closer, extending his arms for a hug, he realized Tan wasn't as thrilled about their reunion as he was.

"What is wrong with you?!" Tan exclaimed. "Have you lost your mind again? You could have blown up my entire operation with your foolishness." She grabbed Selvig's arm and yanked him inside. "If there's one thing I've learned while living in Lil' Odessa, it's *don't mess with Zelda*."

"I transposed the address," Selvig said with a sheepish grin. "I thought I knew it from memory, but I've come to learn that memory can be a funny thing."

Tan turned her attention to Darcy and Felix. "Hello there. Welcome! I swear I don't bite. Come inside, won't you?" She ushered them into her darkened lair. Once inside, Tan flipped a switch and a bright-white light filled the room. The space was stylistically out-of-date. Cheap brown wood paneling covered the walls. Yellow, puddled marks littered the dropped ceiling tiles where rain had seeped in through cracks in the roof. The thin, mangy green carpet was speckled with tiny burn marks. The room was otherwise unfurnished except for an old reclining chair that sat in the middle. Its oddly textured fabric featured a crudely designed woodland scene depicting a cheerful, dancing deer.

Felix looked behind him at the door through which they had entered. "*Uhhhh.* Did we just step through a time machine or is this place a total dump?" he asked.

Tan giggled. "Time machine? Ha! As if time travel were that easy," she said. "For folks like us, it takes more than walking through a doorway to sidestep time and space." Tan walked over to her recliner and plopped herself onto its cushions. She smiled at Felix, looking him up, down, and all around. "I don't know you. Why don't I know you?"

"Felix Desta," he replied. "I'm the new blood."

"*Desta* is Ethiopian, yes?" Tan asked. Felix nodded. "Beautiful country. Borders Wakanda, as I'm sure you know. There's all kinds of new information coming out about the place. That reminds me. I need to look into how that Kimoyo Bead was cataloged." Tan's eyes formed a tight squint as she racked her brain.

"What's a Kimoyo Bead?" Felix asked. "Is that, like, what they give out at Mardi Gras?"

Tan shook her head. "It's advanced Wakandan technology made of vibranium. Capable of information storage, communication, and energy absorption. Don't ask how I got my hands on it, or I'll have to kill you." She winked playfully at Felix, who wasn't sure how to respond. "Eh. I'm sure it'll turn up. It *has* to, right? Tell me, how do you like being Erik's intern? You probably know this by now, but he can be a real pain in the—"

Selvig cupped his hands around Felix's ears. "Please, Anjelica."

"What?!" Tan exclaimed. "Stop being such an old man, Erik." Tan swiveled around in her chair, thinking out loud. "Good interns are so hard to find. I was supposed to have a bunch from some elite magnet schools, but they all bailed at the last minute. Guess they didn't want to get stuck in a basement in the desert all summer. I told them it was air-conditioned! Eh. Their loss." She released an elongated sigh. "So, Felix Desta, did Erik tell you that he and I once—"

Selvig cut off Tan's line of questioning. "*Enough*, Anjelica. Felix is not my intern. Not in an official capacity at any rate. Let it go. We can discuss all this once we're underground."

Tan made an odd noise at Selvig, like a grouchy pet growling at a stranger. She turned her attention to Darcy and softened her demeanor. "You're the glue, huh?" Tan asked. "I've gotta hand it to you, girl. You've got the patience of a saint. If I were in your shoes, I would have bolted a long time ago."

"Have we met?" Darcy asked.

"No," Tan replied. "But you're Darcy Lewis. Erik told me stories. I know your origin, sweetie. I know everyone's origins. It's what I do." Tan settled comfortably into her recliner, leaning back all the way. "Brace yourselves." She pulled a lever on its side.

CUH-CHUNK!

In an instant, the room began shifting as the sounds of metal thrashing filled the air. The wall's wooden panels flipped themselves around to become shining, silver steel. Ceiling tiles folded themselves away, revealing a maze of rods and pistons hanging above.

"And now we're in a trash compactor," Felix said.

Tan stared down Selvig, cocking one eyebrow at him. "Wait a stinkin' minute. Erik, did you not tell them what this place really is?!"

"Nope," Darcy replied, shaking her head. "He didn't say where we were going or why." She put her hand on Selvig's shoulder. "Had to rat you out, dude."

"But you came anyway," Tan said. "Because you, Darcy Lewis, are the glue."

CUH-CHUNK!

The room jolted to a stop. "We're here," Tan said, lifting herself out of her recliner. "Welcome to my bunker. Like I said, it's air-conditioned." The steel walls descended into the floor on all four sides, revealing an expansive underground storage facility. Hundreds of rows of tightly packed metal boxes sat quietly undisturbed. Each box was meticulously numbered and labeled. Some contained classified documents; others contained mysteries and unidentified relics. Tan kept a small open-air office by the door. Her desk was mostly uncluttered. A laptop sat neatly on its surface, along with a mug featuring a tired-looking cat that said STOP STRESSING ME-OWT. Behind the desk was a shelf of miscellaneous items waiting to be returned to their rightful place. One item in particular, a spiked helmet covered in frayed wires, caught Felix's eye. He made his way toward it, his fingertips electric with anticipation.

"*Don't touch that,*" Tan warned.

Felix backed off. "What's in this place?"

"S.H.I.E.L.D. secrets. Mostly."

Felix snickered. "I hate to tell you, but the S.H.I.E.L.D. database was exposed a while back. The whole organization blew up. All their secrets are out there, lady."

Tan relaxed into her office chair and kicked her feet up on her desk. "Kid, I've got paper trails and mission briefs that never made it into that database. You wouldn't understand because your whole world is online. Didn't used to be that way. This place is the premier storage facility for the world's most top-secret reports, testimonies, and chronicles. When everything went digital, organizations like S.H.I.E.L.D. needed a place to put original documents and other items that they just didn't have room for on the Helicarrier."

"Most people shred old documents when they're done with 'em," Darcy said. "Just sayin'."

"I don't just store paper, honey," countered Tan. She gestured to a shelf of boxed items beside her desk. "I've got tech here, too. Storing *that* stuff brings in the big bucks. Better to take dangerous items off the grid than risk them getting stolen by some idiot with mechanical wings."

"You're probably lonely," Felix remarked.

"Eh. Sometimes. Overall? It's not all that bad. When the slow season hits, I watch a lot of Saucy

Sara cooking tutorials on the internet. She's great. Makes a mean sloppy joe." Tan let herself get wistful for a moment, and then she started speaking again. "Plus, I've got an assistant whose company doesn't completely annoy me, so that's something I guess."

"*Yawn*," Felix murmured.

Tan glared at Selvig. "They *really* don't know who I am?!" she roared. "Erik, how much did we go through together, and I don't get a single mention? I'm insulted." Tan pulled up her pant leg to reveal a prosthetic limb. She kicked it up, showing it off to Darcy and Felix. "Got this baby after that dirty business with Loki and the Tesseract, back when I worked with Erik at Project P.E.G.A.S.U.S. One of these days, I'll get around to outfitting it with some bionic enhancements." She paused, perhaps remembering the incident that changed her. "Things didn't go the way any of us planned. That's life, I guess. I decided to take a step back from the full-time scientific hustle and bustle. Astrobiology will always be in my blood, but, for now, being down here suits me okay. Sometimes you just need a break."

"Copy *that*," Darcy said.

Selvig hadn't spoken to Tan in some time. He'd missed her. After the debacle at Project P.E.G.A.S.U.S., he was afraid she might've blamed him for what went down. They'd never actually discussed it. Selvig wanted to express so much but very little came out. "Anjelica," he said somberly. "Recent events have consumed me..."

"They've consumed us all," Tan replied. "Pick yourself up, dust yourself off, and get your head in the game." Tan pointed at a door in the far corner of the facility marked INTAKE. "Felix, Darcy— my assistant will keep you entertained while Papa Selvig and I have a chat."

Darcy and Felix quietly shuffled away. Tan focused her attention on Selvig. "What's up, Erik?" she asked. "What do you need from me?"

"Have you noticed a shift in the cosmos?" Selvig asked.

A devilish grin crept onto Tan's face. "I live

underground cataloging things now, Erik," Tan said. Her eyes revealed there was more to her story than she let on. "It's not as if I've got a web of small, cloaked satellites surrounding the planet that inform me of changes in weather patterns and other strange occurrences. That would be impossible, you see, because when I began this new endeavor, I signed a very detailed S.H.I.E.L.D. document that forbade me from pursuing my astrobiological studies. Conflict of interest or some such. But, as you know, our world gets stranger and more fantastic by the day. Those satellites I don't have? They absolutely did *not* pick up unidentifiable readings before mysteriously erasing themselves and self-destructing. That would be tragic. I definitely am not depressed and confused about it in case you're curious. So, sadly, it seems, I'm of no use. Sorry, old friend." She capped it off with the slyest of winks.

Selvig was humbled by her share. "Thank you for your candor," he replied. "I'm looking for Doctor Jane Foster."

Tan smirked. "Does it look as if she's *here?*"

"It's of the utmost importance that I get in touch with her as soon as possible. Do you know where she might be?"

Tan sighed. "Aruba? Jamaica? Who knows? I'm not her travel agent. You should've filled her bloodstream with tracking nanobots." Selvig was in no mood for jokes. "I don't mean to be insensitive, but Jane may not be anywhere anymore. Half the world just turned to dust...."

Selvig wasn't about to go down that road. "I've considered all the angles," he said. "Jane's work may contain the key to unlocking our understanding of the decimation event."

Tan perked up. "Oh! Well, if it's her work that you need, you're in luck," Tan said. "Wait here." She took off down an aisle and soon returned with a light metal box. "This has Jane's records, atmospheric data, and a couple of doodads from her adventures. You're one of two people who've been granted access, albeit limited in *your* case, by Jane herself."

Selvig opened the box and looked inside. He

moved its contents all around, searching for something he wasn't finding. "Where's her journal? Jane had a leather-bound journal, but it's not here," Selvig said. He grew frustrated. "While we were working together in London, Jane came into contact with an otherworldly power called the Aether. I believe it may be connected to the decimation event Earth recently experienced. Anjelica, *I need that journal.*"

Tan shrugged. "If it's not in that box, I don't know what to tell ya."

Something about Tan's demeanor made Selvig think she knew more than she let on. "I'm desperate, Anjelica," he admitted. "If I'm able to connect the dots, I may be able to get to the bottom of what happened. Help me. *Please.*"

Tan dropped her poker face. She removed a flash drive from a secret compartment located underneath her desk. "This contains Jane's video diaries. I was instructed to keep it away from *anyone* who came looking for it. Telling you it exists, friend of Jane or not, puts me in a difficult position," Tan confided. "I've always believed in you, Erik, despite what you might think. I've always believed in your work and your commitment to the truth. If you're telling me you might be able fix this, I wouldn't feel right not sharing this information. You do understand the difficult position this puts me in, correct?" Selvig nodded affirmatively. "Good. Now come with me." Tan ushered him into a small room containing a flat-screen television, a multimedia player, and two rolling desk chairs. She handed him the flash drive and a tablet. "Put the *thing* in the *thing*. Press PLAY. There are two viewable videos on this thing. Otherwise it's encrypted, so no funny business. *Capiche?*"

Selvig nodded. He was thankful for Tan's help, though he struggled to express it in the moment. "Effective communication hasn't always been my strong suit, as you well know," he said. "Thank you for your assistance in this matter, Anjelica."

"No sweat," Tan said. "Take whatever time you need." She closed the door behind her and returned to her desk where she immediately began to rewatch Saucy Sara's sloppy joe tutorial.

On the other side of the underground facility, Darcy opened the door marked INTAKE. She never in a million years expected to find her ex-boyfriend, Ian Boothby, staring back at her. "You've got to be kidding me," she yelped.

"I saw you come in on the closed-circuit cameras," Ian smirked. He stretched his arms out from his sides, as if to remind Darcy of his shape. He was dressed in jeans and a T-shirt that said R.I.P. EARTH. "I'm alive. Surprised?"

"Nothing surprises me anymore," Darcy replied.

They stared at each other in total silence for roughly thirty seconds. Their brains were brimming with questions they were far too afraid to ask. Their relationship hadn't ended well. It began, however, innocently. Darcy hired Ian the same way Jane had hired her. He didn't have a background in science, but he was cute, funny, and took direction well. They started dating soon after the Convergence event. Try as they might, though, Darcy and Ian just couldn't make it work.

Felix broke the silence and reached out for a

friendly handshake. "I'm Felix," he said. "What do you do here, man?" He sniffed the air. "Besides stink."

"I beg your pardon?" Ian asked.

"Don't mind Felix. He's still learning how to be a real boy," said Darcy.

"I'm the guy who tags and bags stuff once it falls into Anjelica's hands," Ian explained. "It can be boring. And lonely. But it's stability, which is nice, and I've always got the telly to keep me company. There's also a gym down here. One of the perks."

"Ugh," Felix groaned. "No wonder you smell like an underarm."

"That's probably just you going through puberty," replied Ian.

Darcy was impressed by Ian's new physique. "Your arms look like hams. Subterranean isolation does a body good, I guess."

Felix was fixated on the rows of shelves that were filled with boxes waiting to be returned to their proper places. Each one was tagged according to its relevance and placement within the facility. He moved his eyes across them all, noticing names like *the Battle of New York*, *Damage Control*, and *177A Bleecker Street*. Felix's mind raced, imagining the stories and secrets inside each one.

Ian's attention was focused squarely on Darcy. "Still working for Selvig, huh? Some things never change," he muttered.

"Sick burn," Darcy said, rolling her eyes.

Felix quietly removed a stack of files marked *Classified*. The first folder detailed a UFO encounter near Winslow, Arizona, though most of the documents were blacked out. He flipped open another folder and thumbed through a missing-persons report for a woman named Janet Van Dyne.

"Put that back," Ian said.

"Oh. Sorry. You seemed really busy. I thought I'd help with the filing," said Felix, grinning. "Don't worry about paying me. This one is on the house, pal!"

Ian pointed at the shelves. *"Back,"* he said.

Somberly, Felix did as he was told. As he returned the files, he spotted a tiny black ball covered in unfamiliar white symbols, hiding behind a box. He stuffed it into his pocket as slyly as possible.

"Let the kid read a couple of old secrets, dude," Darcy said. "Loosen up."

"Don't distract from the issue, Darcy," protested Ian.

"What *is* the issue, *Ian*?!" Darcy exclaimed.

"You're Selvig's lapdog," Ian said. "When are you going to actually do something for yourself instead of running around doing whatever he tells you?"

Darcy calmed herself as best she could, though Ian's words stung a bit. "Yes, Erik has his moments. He's been through a lot. You were there for some of it! Show some compassion, man. Half the world just crumbled! I'm not leaving the one person who needs me the most."

"The one person who needs you the most?" Ian asked. "That used to be me." He retrieved a gadget from his desk and handed it to Darcy. It was both familiar and outdated.

"This…looks like…my old MP3 player," she said, tilting the device to inspect each of its sides.

"It is," Ian said proudly.

"Okay…but…am I missing something?" Darcy asked. "This was confiscated by S.H.I.E.L.D. back when we first met Thor. Once everyone kissed and made up, they gave it back to me. I still have it somewhere. In a drawer. I think."

"They gave you a decoy made to look exactly like yours. This is the real one. Found it when I was cataloging a bunch of stuff," Ian explained. "I'd ditch the impostor, if I were you. There's a tracking device embedded inside its circuitry. I was going to tell you once I found it but…"

Darcy crinkled her nose. "What a bunch of—" She stopped herself before she said something regrettable. "I can't believe S.H.I.E.L.D. just threw this in a box and put it in storage. That's messed up."

"Maybe they didn't consider you important anymore," Ian said. "That's not to say you *aren't* important. You're a scientist! Or, no, that's not right, you're science-adjacent." He struggled to find his verbal footing. "You know Thor! That makes you a very important person."

"Quit while you're behind," Darcy said, putting the device in her pocket. "Thanks for this, beeteedubs. It'll come in handy on our road-trip-quest thingy."

Ian took a long, deep breath. "What are you looking for?" he asked.

Darcy pondered the question. "Stability. Happiness. I'd love to get a big, dumb dog that I can wrestle around with in the backyard of my farmhouse. Oh, and a farmhouse. I want one of those. Other than that? A job that pays well and allows me to put my political science degree to good use. Not that I don't love what I do *now*, but, you know... It sounds cheesy, but I want to help people. I'd love to be *really* good at that. Those are the broad strokes. Pretty much."

Ian smiled. "No," he said. "I meant what are you looking for on your little road-trip-quest thingy?"

"Oh," Darcy chirped. "The secrets of the universe. Know where we can find some?"

"I'm sure whatever Anjelica gives Erik will help

illuminate things," Ian said, smiling. "Darcy, you're already good at helping people. If I may make a suggestion, though, you may want to learn how to help yourself."

"I'll take that into consideration," she said. Suddenly, her eyes darted around the room in a panic. "Where'd Felix go?"

On the other side of the facility, in the viewing room, Selvig inserted the flash drive and settled into his seat to watch Jane's video diaries.

"Hey," Felix said, arriving unexpectedly. He pulled a chair up next to Selvig and took a seat. "Darcy's ex-boyfriend works at this place. The guy seems like a real tool. Things got kinda weird, so I bolted. Mind if I watch what you're watching?"

"Be my guest," Selvig said. He took the tablet into his hand and pressed PLAY. "Pay close attention, Felix. These tales should illuminate my mission."

"*Our* mission," corrected Felix.

Doctor Jane Foster appeared on the screen, sitting in the manager's office at the Smith Motors

Auto Dealership in Puente Antiguo. She seemed nervous but excited.

"Hello, friend," Selvig whispered. "It's good to see you."

"You know this isn't a live feed, right?" asked Felix.

"*Shhhh!*" Selvig snapped. He swung his index finger up to his lips for added effect.

Felix took the cue and quieted himself.

Jane shifted around in her chair and began her chronicle. *"This is Doctor Jane Foster's video diary regarding the events that took place in Puente Antiguo, New Mexico. I'm, um, Doctor Jane Foster. My colleague, Doctor Erik Selvig, said I should record an account of these events...for posterity...so...here I am. Oh, and if you're watching this because I'm dead, be kind. I'm a scientist not a video blogger."*

"She's funny," Selvig muttered to himself. "I'd forgotten how funny she can be."

"Did you guys used to...you know...date?" asked Felix. "She's cute."

Selvig shot him a dirty look.

"I'm shutting up now."

"I'll begin at the beginning," Jane said. A cell phone rang off camera, and she leaned over to see who it was. *"Ugh. Good ol' Don Blake. Always knows the wrong time to call. You know what? Forget him. Let's get down to business,"* Jane said. *"I'd been studying auroras, tracking magnetic storms, as one does—"*

Selvig pressed fast-forward. "Jane is one of the most brilliant minds of our time, but she'll drone on about the majestic beauty of the auroras for hours if you let her." He patiently waited for an approximate moment to stop. "How about here?"

"—and it was truly one of the most gorgeous sights I'd ever seen in my entire life. Absolutely incredible. I'll drone on about the majestic beauty of the auroras for hours if you let me. Now is not that time." Jane chuckled. *"Anyway, a magnetic storm had erupted in Puente Antiguo. Erik wasn't all that thrilled or impressed. I can hear him now.* You're an astrophysicist, not a storm chaser! *Which is funny considering how our understanding of the universe changed that day."* Jane paused, clearly recalling the exact moment in time

when her work moved to the next level. She shook off the feeling and got back to business. *"What we witnessed in Puente Antiguo was* more *than a magnetic storm. It was an Einstein-Rosen bridge, a* wormhole, *and it spat out the god of thunder."*

"Here we go," Felix said, rubbing his hands together. "The *good* stuff."

"It was startling. To say the least. Thor's a big guy. Cracked the windshield. So, Darcy was freaking out. Erik was whatever..."

"You were just *whatever*?!" exclaimed Felix. "We're talking about *Thor* here, man. I would have lost my head."

Selvig ignored the comment. He wanted to hear more of Jane's recollection.

"My readings were completely off the charts. I'd built all my equipment by hand, and it'd cost me more than I'm willing to admit. That insane storm almost fried every piece. It also left a series of circular markings on the ground, like nothing I'd ever seen. I wanted to stay and study them, but Thor needed medical attention, so we headed to the hospital. But I knew what

we'd seen was a tried-and-true Einstein-Rosen bridge. Erik disagreed. He loves to protest. It's just a theory, Jane! *As if that mattered. Everything is a theory at some point.* Everything. *Then that theory gets proven. He knows that, of course, but maybe he was just afraid that uncovering the truth behind the nature of things might..."*

Felix grabbed the tablet and stopped the video. "Can we talk about Einstein-Rosen bridges for a minute?" he asked. "Jane wrote an article about them in a science journal I read from the library. I made a copy of it. Anyway, she said Thor referred to the wormhole he used to access Earth as the rainbow bridge or Bifrost, but *my* question is—"

Selvig snatched back the tablet from Felix's grasp. "Please, Felix, it's very important that you let me absorb this chronicle uninterrupted." He pressed PLAY as Felix sank into his seat in defeat, mumbling to himself in frustration.

"I needed to talk to Thor. Obviously. Data, readings, measurements; they only tell part of the story. I needed context. Once we realized he didn't just get caught in

the storm, that he was actually inside the thing, experiencing it, we rushed to the hospital to find that he was gone. My smoking gun had disappeared. We got him back. Eventually. But, in the interim, S.H.I.E.L.D. confiscated all my equipment. Agent Coulson said I was a security threat, which was absolutely ridiculous. Thor got my diary back, though, thankfully."

Selvig pressed PAUSE to tell a story of his own. "*I* was the one who rescued Thor," Selvig said proudly. His voice filled with delight. "It was thrilling. To fool his captors, Thor pretended to be Jane's boyfriend. We had it all planned out. I even tossed around falsified identification as if I knew what I were doing. But I didn't! Which was exciting. Thor and I had a bonding moment. I remember our conversation well, despite a few...*impairments.*"

"What do you talk about with a god?" Felix asked. "No offense, but aren't you just a stupid animal to someone like him?"

"No, no, no. God or not, Thor doesn't view humanity like that. Not anymore, at least. At this moment in time, he was unsure of himself and the path ahead," Selvig said. "But anyone who's ever going to find their way in this world must start by admitting they don't know all the answers. The key is to ask the right questions."

"I want to hear more Thories," Felix said. "Get it? *Thor stories?!*"

Selvig was pleased to have Felix along for the adventure and found his humor refreshing. He was in need of a lighter moment. Jane's recollections reminded Selvig that he hadn't always been the supportive mentor he should have been. It left him feeling unsettled. "Jane was convinced Thor was the answer to the mysteries we'd been tracking. *I* thought he was dangerous. She wanted to go after S.H.I.E.L.D. *I* was the one who dissuaded her," Selvig explained. "I should have *believed* her. I should have *supported* her without question. But, you see, the Norse mythology, all these fantastic things, they were just children's stories to me. The electromagnetic storm surges could be explained with ease, but a god who fell from the sky? It didn't make sense. I used to tell Jane that it was our job as scientists to chase every possibility, every alternative. She was doing exactly that! And I still doubted her. I couldn't wrap my head around what I assumed was magic."

"Arthur C. Clarke said, 'Magic is just science we don't understand yet.' You probably already knew that." Felix slowly patted Selvig's shoulder three times in an awkward show of affection. "Cheer up, Doc. That all happened in the past. Don't sweat it. Let's just watch these videos, figure out what we need, and then move forward."

Selvig nodded slowly. "Yes. Yes, yes. That's what we'll do. The information we seek is coming. Let's get prepared." He pressed PLAY and continued.

Jane was smiling. *"Thinking about Thor trying to buy a horse from a pet shop still makes me laugh,"* she said. *"He could have easily treated me like some dumb mortal. I assumed that's what a god would do. But he didn't. He opened up my entire world and took the time to make me feel comfortable. What did I do in return? I kept hitting him with my car. Not an even trade-off. The way he explained the Nine Realms...I'd never*

heard something so incredible. It was all so unbeliev-
able. I had proof that the Einstein-Rosen bridge existed,
but convincing the scientific community to believe me
without an overwhelming amount of hard evidence . . .
wasn't going to be easy."

"That's true," Selvig said, pressing PAUSE. "The scientific community can be so fickle. Science fiction had become science fact very quickly. Jane had broken entirely new ground, and the stubborn gate-keepers didn't know how to handle it."

"My mom and dad were always believers. I mean, *obviously* there's life on other planets. What kind of small-minded little idiot thinks Earth is the only place in the entirety of the cosmos with the conditions to create living things?!" Felix shrugged. "Man, I remember when Thor and the Avengers made their big debut in New York City. Every-thing changed. It was a *big honkin' deal*. The whole world paid attention. I sat in front of the TV for days watching the news and knockin' back bowls of Frosted Sugarbombs. Snatched a red tablecloth and some of my mom's old extensions and ran through the neighborhood telling everyone I was the 'God-uvfunder.' *Ahhh*, to be a kid again."

Selvig snickered.

"What?! I *was* a kid. Comparatively speaking. Even at that age I knew that unexplored worlds meant new biology to study."

Selvig twiddled his fingers as he recalled the excitement of the moment. "It was the first in a chain of events that would totally reshape humanity's understanding of the heavens," he said. "But we still have so much to learn!" He pressed PLAY.

Jane had found her groove. *"While Thor was stuck on Earth, chaos had erupted on Asgard. Thor's brother, Loki, was trying to steal the throne. So then Thor's friends, the 'Warriors Three,' needed him back home to help stop this. Guess how they get to Earth? An Einstein-Rosen bridge! They called it the Bifrost. What I called it was* more evidence to prove my theory." Jane shimmied her shoulder, playfully smirking at the camera. *"Let's see, there was Fandral, Hogun, Volstagg, and Lady Sif."* Jane paused. She appeared confused. *"That's* four *warriors, not three.*

Hmmm. *I suppose Lady Sif is in a class all her own. Actually, I know that for a fact, because I watched her in action, and she is, without a doubt, one of the fiercest women I've ever met. You can quote me on that. Anyway, so, Loki sent something called a Destroyer to kill Thor and take him out of the picture completely. Keep in mind, Thor was totally powerless at this point. He lost his hammer. Darcy called it* Meow-Meow."

"*Meow-Meow?!*" Felix said. "Does she mean Mjolnir? Uh-uh. No way. Unacceptable. You don't go calling one of the greatest weapons in existence *Meow-Meow*! Unless she's talking about something else entirely, and, in that case, I don't want to know."

"*Hearing myself say all this out loud sounds crazy, but* that's what actually happened," Jane said. Her tale was entering into the home stretch. "*Thor confronted the Destroyer who was, well, destroying everything. Poor Puente Antiguo. Loki had been watching the whole thing from Asgard, so Thor made an appeal. 'Take my life and end this!' That's what the Destroyer did. He took his life, or so we thought. I'm embarrassed to admit this, but I was a total mess, crying over Thor's body as if he weren't someone whom I'd just met. But look, the guy had an effect on me, okay? I won't apologize for caring about his welfare. It doesn't matter anyway because he came back to life! His hammer somehow sensed he was in trouble and finally showed up. Next thing we know, Thor is revived and looking like a majestic warrior. He kicked that Destroyer's butt. S.H.I.E.L.D. knew the game had changed, and they had no choice but to change with it. Thor made them give back all my equipment. Coulson wants me to continue my research, so that's an option. As for Thor… he promised me he'd return, and I believe him. As for me…"* Jane appeared to gather her thoughts as they came to her. *"I'm going to expand my resources, publish my findings, and make sure the scientific community understands that this is* just the beginning. *Cosmic forces have been awakened and I'm not about to give up searching for answers to these new mysteries. This has been Doctor Jane Foster's very first video diary. Thanks for watching?"*

Selvig stared at the blank screen, unblinking. Seeing Jane's face and hearing her thoughts stirred something deep within him. The faith he'd lost in the past few months was slowly returning. He felt energized and alive.

"You ever run tests on Mjolnir?" Felix asked. "With the right materials, I bet I could build a reasonable facsimile of that thing in less than a month. Wanna put money on it?"

"It's not possible, I'm afraid," Selvig said. "Though reliving those events through Jane's eyes was fruitful for my process, those particular recollections were not what I was looking for." He brought up the menu and clicked on the next video. "*This* should illuminate things."

Jane looked to be in a S.H.I.E.L.D. facility. She was silent, staring off into the distance. *"This is Doctor Jane Foster.* Again. *Time to talk about the Aether."*

CHAPTER **4**

Selvig had been patiently waiting to hear Jane's recollections about the Aether. She'd spoken to him about it before, but in a more clinical capacity. Selvig hoped that Jane's personal retrospective might yield new information that could aid in the quest.

"Brace yourself, Felix. The Aether is a violent force of nature with no mercy. You may be unsettled by some of these revelations," Selvig warned. "You're about to learn the secrets of the universe, young man. Don't be afraid."

Felix scoffed. "Do I look afraid to you, dude?" Selvig shot him a look. "I'm shutting up now."

Jane exhaled slowly. *"Imagine Erik Selvig, completely naked, on every international news channel, running around Stonehenge,"* she said. *"How's* that *for a start?"*

Selvig scrambled for the tablet. "We need not get into *this,*" he said, fast-forwarding the video. "Let me just…see…what…we…have…here. This should do it."

Felix pinched the skin on his arm. It stopped him from cracking up.

"I'm getting personal. There's no other way to say it. My work and my romantic life happened to overlap. That doesn't mean I can't maintain my professional objectivity. The Einstein-Rosen bridge discovery opened a million doors. I'd begun sharing my work with S.H.I.E.L.D., and they, in turn, helped me try to initiate a portal from Earth to Asgard. Didn't exactly work out. Meanwhile, I didn't know if Thor was even alive. *He promised me he'd return and then… nothing."* Jane appeared uneasy recalling the memory. *"Next thing I knew, Erik Selvig gets kidnapped and telepathically controlled by Loki. Darcy and I are being whisked to Tromsø by S.H.I.E.L.D. for 'our*

protection.' No details, no information, nothing. New York was being attacked by aliens, and our handlers expected us to just go with the flow as if it were no big deal, but it was a big deal. The Avengers saved the planet. When it was over, I assumed Thor might stick around for, I don't know … He went back to Asgard without any notice. …"

"Harsh. To get ghosted by a god? That's *rough*," Felix said. "When does this Aether thing come into play?"

"Give it time," assured Selvig.

Jane was resolute. *"I moved on,"* she said firmly. *"My work was the most important thing. That's what kept me grounded in the real world. I was grateful when Erik invited me to London to investigate a series of gravitational anomalies that had cropped up. He'd been through a lot, and I wanted to be there to support him. Darcy, too. The gang was back together! Except Erik disappeared before I got there."*

"You ghosted her, too? *Dang,"* said Felix. "That's pretty savage, Doc."

Selvig pressed PAUSE. "I wasn't in my right mind,"

he said, flustered. "Loki's Scepter possessed me completely. I was trapped inside my own brain. It was *hellish*. Loki used my gifts in an effort to destroy the planet. You can't possibly understand what that was like!"

Felix squirmed in his seat. "You're right. I don't. Sorry for making a dumb joke, Doctor Selvig. I didn't mean to set you off like that."

"I—I—" Selvig stumbled. He was embarrassed by the raw burst of emotion. "I don't mean to get so upset. My old wounds often feel fresh. I'm learning that the healing process can take a very long time. The struggle, as they say, is real." He paced around the room. "I'd been put into a mental health facility. That's where I *disappeared to*, as Jane said. Darcy and Ian rescued me from that experience and returned me to my work. It was exactly what I needed."

"Ian?! Hold up. He's the lame dude who works here," Felix revealed. "Darcy's talking to him right now."

Selvig hadn't realized Ian was the ex-boyfriend

Felix referenced earlier. "*Hmmm*. Let's not worry about that. It's time we continued on *our* path. The Aether awaits." He pressed PLAY and sat back down.

"*We were on the verge of an incredible break-through. My Phase Meter had picked up on some curious emissions. Darcy, her intern, Ian, and I followed the trail to an abandoned warehouse in London and were confronted with a series of strange phenomena. Small wormholes had opened, seemingly out of nowhere. Laws of physics were breaking down. Gravity was shifting. All in a controlled environment. My Phase Meter went insane. I hadn't seen readings like that since New Mexico. I'm always willing to go the distance for scientific truth, but I had no idea that I'd come face-to-face with one of the most destructive forces in the universe.*"

"*Now* we're talkin'" Felix said, his eyes wide with anticipation.

"*One of the wormholes transported me to what I'd describe as a dark netherworld. It was...absolutely frightening.*" Jane took her time. "*To be alone in a strange place, no way of knowing where you are or how to get home...I wouldn't wish that on my worst enemy. After some panic, I came upon a vault that contained this...presence. A swirling red vapor that* screamed at me. *Like a demon. When I got too close, it attacked me like an infection. I couldn't get it off my skin. Next thing I knew, I was back on Earth. Darcy had called the police while I was gone. At the time I was mad about it. It's not every day you find a stable gravitational anomaly you can study without S.H.I.E.L.D. swooping in and interfering. Oh, and Thor showed up. Of course he did. But anyway, when the police tried to take me into custody, the red netherworld infection just exploded out of my body."* Jane shook her head as if she couldn't believe her own story. *"And that was just the beginning."*

Selvig had worked himself into a frenzy. "Pay close attention, Felix," he said. "At the end of this chronicle, we'll discuss."

"Earthly medicine wasn't going to do the trick, so Thor took me to Asgard. I got to go on the Bifrost. Yes, I should be calling it an Einstein-Rosen bridge. I know." Jane became giddy with excitement. *"But*

this thing was exhilarating *and* unbelievable. *I can be a scientist and still be impressed by majesty."*

"She's perking up." Selvig grinned. "Sadly, it won't last."

*"Asgard's doctors scanned me with a device they called a Soul Forge. It was really just a Quantum Field Generator, but 'Soul Forge' has a fun ring to it, doesn't it? Anyway, Odin told me I wasn't welcome in Asgard. I was just a dirty human. When his guards tried to grab me, the red infection attacked them. Seeing that changed Odin's opinion of me and my affliction. He knew its name—*the Aether. *Odin described it as an engine of infinite destruction. An ever-changing fluid that sought out host bodies and devoured their souls. I'd come to find out later it was one of six unique cosmic forces. Regardless, no one knew how to get it out of my body."*

"Six cosmic forces." Selvig gasped. "I don't believe I ever knew that...."

"Odin told me that, in ancient times, the leader of the Dark Elves, Malekith, used the Aether to reign supreme. It was his ultimate weapon against King Bor

and the forces of Asgard. In the heat of battle, as the Nine Realms converged, Malekith sought to unleash the Aether's full potential but was stopped by the Asgardians. They defeated him, or so they thought. Actually, Malekith went into hibernation while the Asgardians buried the Aether in a place they believed would never be found." Jane's lips formed a half smile. *"Lucky me. When the Aether reawakened, so did Malekith and the Dark Elves. Perfect timing with the Convergence just around the corner..."*

Selvig's eyes lit up. He quickly paused the video. "Felix, take note. There are nine realms in the cosmos—Asgard, Jotunheim, Svartalfheim, Vanaheim, Nidavellir, Niflheim, Muspelheim, Alfheim, and Midgard, otherwise known as Earth. Every five thousand years the realms align themselves, causing all sorts of disastrous phenomena. Gravity swells! The crashing together of light and dark matter!"

"Sounds crazy," Felix said, quizzically rubbing his chin. "But, theoretically, wouldn't you be able to pinpoint an epicenter and find a way to stabilize all that activity?"

"Perceptive!" exclaimed Selvig. "Precisely why I created a set of Gravimetric Spikes to do just that. Stay tuned." He pressed PLAY.

"Malekith came for the Aether. He attacked Asgard and killed Thor's mother, Frigga, during the invasion. I saw my first—and hopefully last—Asgardian funeral. People traveled from the far reaches of the cosmos to pay their respects. It was so moving, so powerful, so…" She trailed off. *"It was a celebration of Frigga's unstoppable spirit."*

Selvig smiled. *"Frigga,"* he whispered. "Like a fairy tale."

It was clear that Jane had become tired of telling this story. She pushed through as best she could. *"So! Malekith didn't get the Aether. Cheers to little victories. I, however, was still stuck on Asgard, stricken with sickness. The Aether took control of my senses and appeared to me as a chaotic mass of churning thunder. It was* intoxicating. *And terrifying. I felt its power in every part of myself—body, mind, and soul. It was killing me."*

A pit had grown inside Selvig's stomach. "Jane

and I have been colleagues for many years. Before that, her father and I taught at Culver together for decades. I made a vow to myself that after he passed, I'd always support her. Sometimes I can't help but feel as if I've—" Selvig stopped himself before finishing the sentence. He was afraid that speaking the words would make them true.

"I've followed Doctor Foster's career for a long time. Ever since I was, like, six. How did I never know she went through all this mess?" he asked, shaking his head. *"This is crazy."*

Jane had reached her breaking point. *"Okay, look, I understand that this chronicle needs to be complete, but I'll be honest, I'm exhausted. Here are the broad strokes—Thor, Loki, and I escaped Asgard together to confront Malekith. I can still see Loki's smirk. He wanted the Aether's power so bad. As if he'd even be able to handle it. We ended up on Svartalfheim, and, after a whole bunch of trickery, Malekith sucked the Aether from my body and absorbed it into his. The sickness was gone. My life was saved. I wish I could say that was the end. But it's not. Not by a long shot.*

The Convergence was happening. Malekith was heading to Earth while Thor and I were stuck in a cave in Svartalfheim. We discovered a portal and got out of there as quickly as possible. Time was running out. Malekith was going to fire the Aether where all nine worlds were aligned. The fallout would have been catastrophic if not for one thing: science!" She thought for a moment and changed her posture. *"Actually,* two *things: science and* Erik Selvig."

Felix pumped his fist in the air. "Legend status: unlocked."

"Erik pinpointed Greenwich, England, as the epicenter of the Convergence, so that's where we headed. Without his invaluable work on Gravimetric anomalies as well as his Gravimetric Spikes, I don't know what we would've done. The walls between worlds were breaking down. Gravity was increasing and decreasing at a rapid rate. The laws of physics had gone bonkers. Don't get me started on the spatial extrusions. Reality was being ripped to shreds and then came Erik Selvig, ready to save it. Darcy was there, too. And Ian. I forgot about him for a second. There was also

this giant creature called a Jotunheim beast that came through a portal." She caught herself getting distracted. "Focus, *Foster."*

"A Jotunheim beast!" exclaimed Felix. "I'm bookmarking that one."

"Malekith arrived and we set up the Gravimetric Spikes in formation. They'd been designed to detect *anomalies, but, after a few tweaks, we used them to increase the gravitational forces, exploiting the fragile spots between universes and thusly* causing *anomalies that transported the Dark Elves...let's just say,* elsewhere. *Thor beat Malekith and took the Aether back to Asgard where it was locked up for safekeeping."* Jane's expression turned grave. *"But the Aether changed me.* Physically. *It invaded my corporeal form. My essence. My* soul. *I need to take some time away to heal, but there's one final thing...something I need to get off my chest..."* Jane hesitated. *"Gonna save that for next time."*

The video ended, and Selvig's mouth fell open. "What the devil? No cliffhangers! Jane said the Aether was one of *six cosmic forces.* We've yet to hear about the other five. One would assume that information is contained in an additional video. But Anjelica said there were only two here!" He grabbed the tablet and furiously pressed its buttons.

"No. Don't do that, Doc. You look desperate," Felix warned. He swiped the tablet out of Selvig's grip and began pressing its buttons at lightning speed. "Taught myself how to hack when I was wearin' diapers." With a final keystroke, he'd accessed encrypted data and handed it back to Selvig. "You're welcome." Another video soon began to play.

Jane's face appeared looking rested and healthy. *"Hello again. This will be my last diary entry before I hand over my material to Anjelica Tan. I need a few things on the record. About Thor."*

"Uh-oh." Felix gulped. "Man, now this feels *wrong.*"

"I'm proud of what we had. We did the best we could with the hand we were dealt. Did I expect us to be able to go out to a restaurant and hit the club on a Saturday night? Of course not. I didn't even want that. The truth is, Thor and I had different paths and different expectations. We cared a lot about each other

but—" Jane stopped herself. *"We were meant for other things. That's as plain as I can put it."*

She paused again.

"There's something else that's been on my mind. A matter I haven't fully investigated. During my time on Asgard, I browsed through Odin's library and found a book about a set of powerful items that, if wielded together, could control the universe. I assumed it was a story, but I've since become convinced that we are all in great danger..."

The door to the viewing room swung open. Anjelica Tan wasn't pleased.

"WHAT. DID. I. SAY?!" she shouted.

Selvig scrambled to cover. "Anjelica, the archive was incomplete! You must understand," he pleaded. *"The archive was incomplete."*

Tan yanked the flash drive out of its socket and took back the tablet. "It's time for you to go, Erik," she said, staring at Selvig with disappointment in her eyes.

"Miss Tan?" Felix said sheepishly.

"Doctor Tan..."

Felix nodded dutifully, embarrassed by his slip of the tongue. "Doctor Tan, I'm sure you know how it is when you're so focused on results that you'll do anything to prove your point—even if it means engaging in decryption."

Tan raised her palm. She'd heard enough. "Save the smooth talk, kid. I was sure the code was solid. The fact that you hacked it is quite impressive, but it also gets under my skin." Tan turned her attention to Selvig. "Erik, I know you've been through a lot, and it hasn't been easy for your mind to heal. Take a step back, my friend. Get some clarity. You need it."

"I appreciate your support, Anjelica," Selvig said. "Thank you for aiding in my research. I apologize for abusing your trust."

Tan smirked. "It's not the first time. Learn a lesson for once, would you? But, yeah, you need to go now." She escorted Felix and Selvig to the exit, talking as they walked. "Where you headed next?"

Selvig squinted and squirmed. He was reluctant to reveal the exact destination.

"Oh fine! Keep your mouth shut," Tan said. "I

guess I won't tell you who's planning a big thing that you'll definitely want to know about."

"What does that mean?!" Selvig asked.

"What do you *think* it means?!" Tan shot back.

Selvig wanted to know, so he revealed where they'd be headed. "Anoki," he blurted out.

"Bwa-ha-ha-ha-ha-ha!" Tan cackled. "Good luck with that one."

"Who's Anoki?" Felix asked.

The trio had arrived at the front of the facility, where Darcy and Ian had been waiting patiently. Darcy poked Felix in the chest. "Thanks for abandoning me," she said.

Felix rolled his eyes. "Thanks for involving me in your boyfriend drama," he said.

"He's not my—" Darcy was done with the conversation. "There's no drama, okay."

Meanwhile, Selvig wasn't about to let Tan off the hook. "Out with it, Anjelica," he demanded.

"Your old friend Ignatius Bixby is throwing a party of some kind. I got a 'save the date,'" Tan declared.

Ignatius Bixby. The name made Selvig's blood boil. "That man is not my friend! He is a fraud!"

Tan leaned into Felix's ear. "They've got beef," she whispered. "You know, with science."

"Ignatius Bixby? *Iggy* Bixby?! The infomercial guy!" Darcy exclaimed. "My mom loves him."

"He's a patent snatcher. Takes someone else's great idea, cheapens it, and then makes a gazillion dollars," Tan explained. "He's done it with robots, vaccines, kitchen appliances, you name it. Apparently, he's gathering the scientific community together for some announcement. I don't know anyone who's going, but *you* might want to check it out."

Selvig pretended to spit. "Never," he said.

"Suit yourself," Tan said. "Keep in touch and all that. You know where to find me." She suddenly remembered something. Tan ran over to her desk and flung open a drawer. After a few seconds of rummaging, she stopped, shaking her head with dismay. "I wanted to give Felix a tiny piece of Arnim Zola's burned-out circuitry as a little souvenir but, truthfully, I forgot where I put it. Oh well."

Tan shrugged. "There's a diner a few blocks away. Go get yourselves something to eat before you take off. If you're heading to Anoki's, you'll need some energy for the climb."

"I'm sorry, but did you say *climb*?" Darcy asked.

"Be careful out there," warned Tan. "The world is an unpredictable place."

Selvig, Darcy, and Felix stepped into the elevator and bade good-bye to Tan and Ian.

"What did she mean by climb?"

CHAPTER 5

"*Ugh*," Felix groaned, holding his belly as if preparing to give birth. "I feel like an alien is about to explode out of my stomach." He'd just finished eating a cheeseburger, fries, a side salad, a bowl of chicken noodle soup, and a triple-scoop ice cream sundae. "If I die, donate my body to science," he said with a whimper.

"Told you not to have that salad," Darcy joked.

"The appropriate term is extraterrestrial, Felix. Not *alien*. If you want to be taken seriously, proper terminology is very important." Selvig's tone was unusually stern. The humiliating experience at the Dollar Holler, coupled with Anjelica Tan's scolding, left him feeling on edge. He assumed a nice bite to eat, some light conversation, and a comfortable environment might ease his mind. Thus far, that wasn't the case.

"Erik, I've heard you use the word *alien* a million times," said Darcy.

Selvig pursed his lips and narrowed his eyes. "I need fresh air," he said, removing himself from the booth. His head hung low, Selvig stomped outside like a child who had just been told to go to his room.

"Guess I'm payin'," Darcy said, glancing at the check. *"Again."*

Felix had known Selvig for only a short time, but he'd seen the man's intelligence at work and wondered if there was any way to help him get through his funk. "Be real with me, Darcy. I know we just met, and I know you think I don't know anything about Doctor Selvig, but I've been studying him. His behavioral patterns and stuff. Sometimes he is *so chill*. We'll hang out like I am one of his boys. Other times he's a total scatterbrain, babbling about one thing then switching to another. I like the guy; don't get me wrong." Felix looked over both his shoulders to make sure Selvig wasn't close by. "But I'm worried he's losing it."

Darcy knew the feeling all too well. "Yeah," she

said, pausing to consider the situation. "Loki's Scepter really did a number on his head. He was better for a while. Looked as if everything was good to go. Then the decimation happened, and he started breaking again."

"We have to get him back on track," Felix said.

"Easier said than done. You're not going to like hearing this, but I've worked for Erik Selvig for a while now. I could tell you things about him he doesn't know about himself. If there's one thing I've learned, it's that he likes to figure stuff out on his own. He's not always receptive to help."

"Stubborn? *Pshh.* I've dealt with worse," said Felix.

"All I'm saying is, don't be surprised if he pushes you away," Darcy said.

"If he pushes people away, why are *you* still here?"

"The dental benefits," Darcy replied. She played with her straw, nervously twirling it with her fingers. "Look, Erik will be fine." She took a long slurp from her soda. "Hopefully."

"That story about Thor, Jane, and the Aether is wild. I'd seen clips online—news reports and stuff—but I never knew the real deal."

"Erik never told you about it before? *Hmm.* I guess you two aren't the science bros you thought you were."

"Is that supposed to make me jealous? You really think I'm that petty? Well, here's a little personal tea for you," Felix said. "I still can't believe I've even met him. When he checked in at the Seafarer, I straight up lost my mind. It was crazy. Statistics are *not* my thing, but the most admired astrophysicist on the planet showing up at the motel I just *happen* to be living in? The chances of that occurring are—"

"Cosmic?"

"Something like that."

"Explain to me how a baby face like you was able to stay at a motel all by himself."

"What can I say? I'm slick." Felix smirked. "Half the tenants disappeared. I filled a vacancy. Dumb Ken didn't ask any questions. All he wanted was to get paid. I kept to myself. Figured I'd try to make it out to California on my own. There's this school I read about. I started saving money for a bus ticket. Worked at night, schooled myself during the day. I'd hear Erik talking to himself, spouting out scientific theories whenever I'd walk by his room. One day I knocked. He let me in, and we kicked it for an entire afternoon. Mostly, he talked, and I listened. He wasn't entirely clearheaded but that didn't matter. Dude is mad intelligent. He said if the decimation can happen, everything we've known is a lie and nothing matters anymore."

"Dark," Darcy murmured. "You've been through a lot, kid. I gotta give you props. I'd probably crawl up in a ball if I, you know, went through all that."

"I'm not as scarred as you think I am."

"I didn't mean—"

Felix shook his head. "I'm not a child."

"We've know each other less than a day. Chill."

Felix pounded his fist on the table. "I need answers, too! The universe will not control my destiny. *I will!*" His anger swiftly fell away as a random thought entered his brain. "Do you think the Aether might be a Radical Quantum Selector?"

"Can we not talk about science for *one minute*?" Darcy whined. "Seriously. The world has gone insane and our dear leader is"—she looked outside to find Selvig seemingly arguing with himself—"hanging by a thread. Meanwhile, we're headed to the mountains to meet an Anoki. For some reason. I'm getting tired. I don't know if this is all leading to the grand revelation he thinks it's leading to. So, please, change the subject. I need to talk about something meaningless. Like reality TV or makeup."

Felix's studied Darcy's face. "You don't wear makeup."

"I would if I had the chance to talk to people about it!" Darcy countered. "Prodigy or not, isn't there other stuff relevant to a twelve-year-old? Like candy? Or toys?"

"*That's* what you think I care about?" Felix said, rolling his eyes. "Why don't you just ask me what I'm going to be for Halloween?"

"What *are* you going to be for Halloween?" asked Darcy.

"*Uggghhh,*" Felix said, slumping down in his seat.

"You don't know yet, do you? Totally been there. Vampires are lame. Witches are out. I get it. Why not go as Iron Man? I hear he's all the rage," Darcy said. Felix sat up, preparing to leave. "Sit back down for, like, one minute. I'm just giving you a hard time." Felix slid back into the booth. "But, seriously, what do you think of that Iron Man, huh? He's cool, right?"

"Yeah, Stark is cool," Felix said. "But I like Doctor Foster better."

"Yeah. Me too." Darcy remembered something. "She has my favorite hat. *Had* my favorite hat? *Yeesh.* I don't want to think about this right now."

Felix fished around in his pockets, pulling out a crumpled wad of lint, a piece of scrap paper, and some change. He peeled the mess apart to find a ten-dollar bill. He pushed it in Darcy's direction.

"Put your money away. This one's on me," Darcy said, noticing a newspaper clipping wedged into the messy bunch of items. She fished it out and brushed it off. "These are your parents, huh?"

"Yeah," Felix said warmly as he gazed at the

image. In it, he and his parents stood in front of the New York Hall of Science, accepting a grant to fund their research. "Science. It's in our blood."

"Literally."

TAP, TAP, TAP.

Selvig's finger pressed against the diner window. He anxiously swept himself through the parking lot, waving his arms in a wild formation, mouthing the words *let's go* over and over again.

We're coming, Darcy mouthed back. "Get a grip, man."

The waitress sauntered over to the table to retrieve the paid check. "All y'all have been nice and everything, but you need to get your friend," she said, pointing to Selvig. "He's freakin' out the other customers."

"He freaks us out, too, ma'am. Apparently, that's just what he does now. Thanks for the hospitality!" Darcy said. "On to our next destination."

―――――――――――

"It's up here. Up ahead!" Selvig said, waving his index finger in all directions. "Up, up, up! Stop dawdling!" Darcy and Felix found themselves hiking through the Sangre De Cristo Mountains. It was the last thing they wanted to do. The sun was bright, the air was fresh, and the sound of birds chirping filled the sky. For the moment, at least.

"You could've called this Anoki person," Darcy said, digging her foot into a rocky outcropping. "You could've said, *Hey, old friend! Know where Doctor Foster is, by chance?* It would've saved us a very annoying trek up a mountain."

"Anoki is without a phone. A brilliant mind, there is no doubt, but one that has chosen to forsake some modern comforts in favor of natural living," said Selvig. "We've a much bigger calling now, Darcy. This trek has filled my brain with new stimulus. Our mission is expanding."

"Perfect. The *Mary Jackson* will love hearing that."

During his time at Culver University, Selvig mentored only a handful of students. Few were as gifted as Anoki. Entering the Theoretical Astrophysics program is no easy task, but Anoki went above and beyond, winning grants, awards, and accolades all before the end of sophomore year. They were humble about it, if also a bit shy. Selvig found them to be brilliant, engaging, and curious. He pressed Anoki to keep going, though, in the end, it wasn't meant to be. Anoki's goal was always personal growth. Science was simply a fascination. Anoki dropped out of school and invented an app that allowed travelers to plan getaways based on a weather-prediction system. It made so much money they decided to cash out quickly and begin a new chapter away from modern civilization. Though supportive, Selvig didn't take the news of Anoki's early retirement very well.

CRACK-A-THOOM!

A surprising thunderclap echoed through the sky, followed by a flash of lightning. Dark clouds suddenly moved in as droplets of water quickly turned to torrents.

"We're doomed," Darcy said. She closed her eyes and let the water drench her completely.

"I love it," Felix said, extending his arms out from

his sides, as if the rainfall renewed him in the midst of an exhausting climb.

Selvig spotted a cavern in the hillside. "This way!" he shouted.

Darcy, Felix, and Selvig made their way into the empty cavern and dried off. It was deep and littered with old animal carcasses. The three of them walked as far as the light would allow.

"*Hmmm*," Selvig murmured. "I assumed *this* was Anoki's home, but it doesn't look as if anyone lives here."

Darcy gently kicked a raccoon skull out of her way. "Not unless they're tampering in dark-sided stuff," she joked. "Does this Anoki do ritual sacrifices? If that's the case, I'll head back to the car."

Selvig corrected Darcy's notion. "These bones are part of the life cycle of the forest," he said. "Anoki does not perform ritual sacrifice. At least, not that I know of."

"*Errriiik?*" A lilting voice called out from the edge of the cave. "Tell the spirits why you've come here today...."

"Uh, this is weird," Felix said.

"Who goes there?!" Selvig exclaimed. "Show yourself!"

Anoki's tall, thin frame, draped in a long, intricately designed poncho, seemed to float into the cavern. Their face was bright, caramel, and expressionless. Their waist-length silky black hair jostled back and forth in the wind. Anoki's warm blue eyes pierced Darcy's soul.

"Oh...my..." she said softly.

"Good evening," Anoki said with a slight grin. "Did you think some dark force had come to get you, Erik? Is that why you're yelling? It's nice to know I haven't lost the ability to throw my voice. I never get to use that skill. How entertaining it is to watch you squirm."

"Hello, Anoki," Selvig said, relieved. "How did you know we were here?"

"My great ancestors whispered to me in my dreams," Anoki said. "Kidding. I heard you screeching up the mountain a mile away, barking orders at your poor underlings. It felt very *familiar*. Like how you used to bark at me during my freshman year whenever I was late to class."

"*Time is fluid* was a poor excuse," said Selvig.

"Yet not an untrue statement. Time *is* fluid, like so very many things in this world, including gender. Obviously," Anoki replied. "My encampment is nearby. It's covered. Come. I'll make some tea." Anoki motioned for the trio to join and they walked to a cool, dry place.

———————————————

"Welcome. Your clothes will dry momentarily," Anoki said, entering the tree house. The area was spacious, circular in shape, and decorated with cloth wall hangings, large beanbag chairs, and gigantic pillows. There were shelves of spices, stacks of books, and baskets of fresh vegetables waiting to be eaten. Spread throughout the space was an assortment of crystals and geodes, each one carefully placed. In the corner, a spigot provided running water. There wasn't a single piece of technology in sight.

"Why are you and your associates here, Erik?"

Anoki asked, relaxing on a chaise lounge. "Let's do away with pretense."

"Very well. We're looking for Doctor Jane Foster," Selvig replied.

"She's not *here*," said Anoki. "Are you sure that's why you've come all this way? Don't be shy, Erik. Is this *really* about Doctor Foster?"

Selvig groaned. "Your response is unhelpful."

"Well then, how about this one? Half the planet turned to ash. Consider, for a moment, that Doctor Foster's physical form is no longer with us. Consider that her body has perished, and her spirit has ascended into a greater realm. That may help lift whatever burden you're carrying."

"Don't be cruel, Anoki," Selvig said.

"I wasn't. I'm simply making an educated guess and a polite suggestion," Anoki said. "What's your theory *du jour* on the decimation?"

Selvig exhaled. "Earth has experienced a great deal of trauma...."

Anoki scoffed. "Ha! Tell me about it."

Selvig bristled. Anoki's sarcasm left him feeling

unprepared. "I'm still assembling the pieces. However, I believe recent phenomena have put the planet in a perilous position. I seek a greater understanding of these events and their connection to the cosmos."

"Already I can see you're not utilizing all your resources," Anoki said. "Why are you *here* and not at the Water of Sight?"

Selvig's face turned red. Years ago, he shared a story with Anoki about a strange and ancient body of water he'd visited with Thor. It was hidden away from the world and possessed immeasurable cosmic abilities. Selvig told Anoki never to mention it again. Anoki, however, was never one to follow orders. "As I have explained to you, in the past, the Water of Sight is far too powerful a thing. It's unpredictable. There's no way to use it safely. That is the bottom line. I do not wish to speak of it."

Anoki was taken aback. "I've never known you to fear something like this before, Erik. Should I be worried or disappointed?" they asked. "Instead of focusing on these cosmic games, perhaps you should focus on healing yourself first?"

"I'm *fine*," Selvig said. "I've merely sensed a great cosmic imbalance is all."

"Join the club!" Anoki exclaimed. "The web of life, the fabric of existence was meddled with beyond comprehension. If you really want answers, go where you can get them."

Darcy and Felix looked at each other with shared confusion.

Anoki's eyes widened. "Ah! You always like a bit of gossip," they said, poking Selvig in the side. "Ignatius Bixby is apparently having a party for a thing. He had a drone bring me an invitation. Can you believe?"

"I'm not going," Selvig replied flatly.

"Didn't get an invite, huh? Poor baby," Anoki said with a giggle. "Boy, oh boy, is Bixby jealous of you, Erik."

"Ha!" Darcy yelped. "I mean . . . um . . . why?"

Anoki gestured toward Selvig. "This is a brilliant, complicated man of science. Flawed, as all things are, but respected, admired. His opinions are deeply considered. They have value within the community.

Bixby, however, became a neuroscientist for two reasons: number one, his own vanity, and number two, manipulating minds. He's an ignorant, shallow charlatan. He never built himself a body of work, so, instead, he became a lame television personality. He'll attach his name to a blender if you pay him. Earning *wealth* became his goal. Now he's trying to dunk on you, Erik, as my basketball-loving father might say. This *soiree* is his way of letting you know he's thriving and you're not."

Selvig grimaced.

"Ignore my opinion at your own peril," Anoki said. "But, at the moment, his wealth might provide you with resources. Personally speaking, I wouldn't go to that party if you paid me. Yes, I know I'm rich beyond measure, but you get what I'm saying. Ignatius Bixby is a low-rent Tony Stark, which isn't saying much, considering Stark is a capitalist in a cheap suit of gaudy armor."

"They're hardly comparable, Anoki. Are you mad? Stark is a brilliant man. He can be a stubborn egomaniac—"

"Said the pot to the kettle…"

"Will you let me finish?" Selvig persisted. "Despite his human flaws, Stark respects science. He cares about *people*. He cares about *the future*."

"He cares about *money*."

"Yes, he does. We all do! You may live among the trees, but let's not pretend you're without means," Selvig said.

"My road to success wasn't paved with gold, as you well know. I fought for what I have," replied Anoki. "What do *you* fight for these days?"

"I fight for logic. I fight for reason. I fight for proof. I'm fighting for the truth of our very existence!" Selvig exclaimed.

"That's the spark I remember." Anoki smirked. They took a moment to realign. "You, Erik, need to reconcile your mind. Clarity will refine your true purpose."

Selvig became agitated. "How do you suppose I do that, eh? Should I see a therapist? Shall I make a doctor's appointment?!" Selvig's tone shifted to mockery. "Hello, Doctor? I just haven't felt the same since Loki, the Asgardian god of mischief, used an otherworldly Scepter to control my actions. I hurt people. *Friends.* The thought still gnaws at me. I often go to bed at night wishing I would've never become involved with these *Super Heroes*. Doctor, might you be able to prescribe me something to deal with the aftereffects?"

"That would've been a start," Anoki said. They rose from their perch and prepared some tea. "Erik, you supported me and my education when others wouldn't. Without your guidance, I wouldn't have been able to create the conditions that allowed me to live comfortably, on my own terms. I'm forever grateful," they said kindly. "If you think for one minute I'm going to stand by and let you give me this pathetic excuse, you've got another thing coming. Your mind is a gift! Heal it. Protect it! It's time to come through the darkness and into the light." Anoki handed over a mug. "*This* is the way. We both know it's the real reason you're here."

Selvig glared at the tea suspiciously. It was thick, black, and smelled pungent. He didn't want to drink it, but he trusted Anoki's counsel. "Down the hatch," he said, gulping the mixture completely. *"Blech!"* He scraped his tongue with his fingertips. "Tastes like gasoline."

"So *dramatic*, Erik," Anoki said. "Let go of the past, and acknowledge that you cannot stop the future."

Selvig began to sweat. His body tensed as he fell to his knees, out of breath.

"Boss?" Darcy said. "You okay?"

"I'll be fine," Selvig said. "Better soon, hopefully."

Anoki helped him onto the chaise lounge. "Rest. When you wake, your burden will have lifted," Anoki said, fluffing a small woven pillow and putting it behind Selvig's head. "Won't that be nice?"

"What did you give him?" Darcy asked.

"Calm yourself," Anoki said, lighting a sprig of sage. "He drank an ancient medicinal brew that will help heal his mind and renew his spirit. That's all you need to know. Now that he's out, the three of us can talk shop."

The smoke from the sage stung Darcy's nostrils,

making her cough. "You should check out Dollar Holler," she said, waving the soot away from her face. "They've got an amazing selection of incense—strawberry, wasabi, urinal cake. You'll love it. So much nicer than whatever this stuff is."

Anoki rolled their eyes. "A comedian. What a treat," they said, waving the glowing herbs in a circular motion. "This is called smudging. It's a ritual that's meant to cleanse an area of negative energy. Get used to it. Hanging around with the good doctor can be a real drag."

Darcy smirked. "I take the good with the bad." She glanced around the dwelling. "So, are you, like, a survivalist? One of those people who stock up on buckets of taco meat because they think the world is ending?"

"That's *exactly* who I am," Anoki said, entertained by the thought. "You're a clever one, Darcy Lewis."

Darcy froze. "I didn't tell you my name," she said, her voice panicked.

"You're the glue," Anoki said. "That much is clear."

"Why do people keep saying that?" Darcy asked. She watched Anoki dig into their satchel to retrieve a touch screen tablet. "That's some real off-the-grid living, right there."

"*Very* primitive," Anoki said.

"Erik told us you don't have a phone," said Felix.

Anoki cackled. "*Ha-ha-ha-ha!* Who doesn't have a phone?! What a grotesque thought," they said, swiping their finger across the tablet and offering it to Darcy for inspection. It was a photo of her and Ian. "This is *you*, yes? And your ex-suitor."

Darcy grabbed the device, flipping through a file with her name on it. She was shocked to find photos, documents, and a treasure trove of her personal information. "Wh-what th-the?!" she stuttered, breathless. "It takes a lot to scare me, okay? I've seen a monster from another dimension rip apart London."

"*It was a Jotunheim beast*," reminded Felix.

"All *this*? It's really freaking me out right now. Make it go away, please," Darcy said, handing the tablet back to Anoki. "Why do you have my life story readily available?"

"Erik and I have had our share of quarrels over the years, but we've always kept in touch. To a degree. He values my opinion, so when you entered into his world, a stranger with no scientific background, I did the due diligence," Anoki explained. "I'm the reason you have a job, sweetie. A thank-you would be nice."

"Erik didn't hire me. Jane did," Darcy replied. *"From the internet."*

"That's correct," Anoki said. "But how do you think you were able to stay in your position? Especially when there are so many who are more qualified. You'd still be trolling for jobs on *the internet* if it weren't for my wise counsel."

"I don't believe you," Darcy said.

Anoki rolled their eyes. "Of course you don't," they said. "Neither does Erik. But my intentions are honorable, despite what he may have told you."

"He doesn't tell us anything," replied Darcy.

"Well, then, you should know I'm amazing," Anoki said, grabbing an apple from the fruit basket and taking a bite. "We have a bit of time to kill before he wakes up. Anything on your mind?"

"You know Loki's Scepter isn't all that unbelievable, right?" Felix asked. "I mean, I know it messed with Doctor Selvig's head, but..." His nose scrunched as he tried to communicate his ideas. "The brain runs on electricity. It controls the flow of ions and sends electrical signals from neuron to neuron. Whatever that Scepter is, it changed the electrical currents in his brain, which, in turn, controlled his brain function, thereby allowing him to become susceptible to intense suggestion. It's, like, crystal clear. Everyone thinks it's some magical thing but it's *so much more simple* than all that. Know what I mean?"

"What was *your* name?" Anoki asked. "I don't have a file on *you*."

"Felix. Last name Desta," he responded. "Write it down. Tell your friends."

"So self-assured, you are. I imagine you see yourself as the next Erik Selvig, yes?"

Darcy chimed in: "Actually, he sees himself as the next Jane Foster."

"A fine choice."

"You're both wrong," Felix replied. "I don't plan on being 'the next' anyone. I'm the first *me*."

"Very astute, Felix Desta," Anoki said. "Where do you study? One of those science high schools?"

"I'm kind of in between schools at the moment."

Anoki considered Felix's situation. "I have a friend who's an instructor at the Wakandan Outreach Centre. It's fast becoming the place to be for young minds like yours. They'd be lucky to have you."

Before Felix could react, Darcy noticed Selvig's chest expanding and contracting at a quicker pace.

"What's going on with him right now?" she asked.

"That Scepter stole a piece of his soul. I'm helping him get it back," Anoki explained.

"By poisoning him?" Darcy asked.

"His recovery plan clearly hasn't been enough," Anoki said. "He requires a medicinal push. Thankfully, he has *me* to give it to him."

"Gah!" Selvig yelped as he tossed and turned. His eyes closed tightly and he began his spiritual journey.

"Wake up, you pathetic, dawdling, flesh bag," a

voice hissed in Selvig's ear. He opened his eyes to find Loki sneering at him from across the room. Darcy, Felix, and Anoki were nowhere to be found. Selvig patted down each of his limbs. He slapped himself across the face.

Loki rolled his eyes. "Have you concluded your investigation?" he asked. "Are you really here, or am I a figment of your imagination? What's the verdict?"

Selvig remained silent. He wasn't sure what was happening yet.

Loki snapped his fingers as the elements of Ano-ki's home slowly fell away, piece by piece. "Apparently, you're one of the most brilliant men on this planet, which begs the question, why haven't you done what you know needs to be done?" Loki asked. *"Hmm?"* The walls were gone. The floorboards soon followed. Loki snapped his fingers again. The Scepter appeared, floating in the middle of the space. The glowing stone that once powered it had been removed and replaced with a drab gray pebble. "Are you afraid *now*, Erik?"

Selvig rose to his feet. "No," he said firmly. "Your weapon is without its power source, and I cannot be controlled by it."

"Are you sure?" Loki said playfully.

The drab gray pebble exploded, sending slivers of stone in all directions. Selvig threw his arm up to protect his face. When he lowered it, the Scepter had grown twice its size. It had also gained a new, familiar power source.

"That—that stone . . . that's what you used to control my mind," Selvig stammered. He slowly backed away from the device.

"This old thing?" Loki said, swiping the Scepter and twirling it through the air like a baton. "Don't worry, Erik, it's not as if it can control you. You said it yourself." Loki violently jabbed it in Selvig's direction.

"No!" Selvig exclaimed. He swerved, lost his footing, and fell to the ground. Selvig was so focused on the Scepter that he hadn't noticed his surroundings had completely transformed. They were now on a small, cold planetoid. Swirling gas giants glowed in the sky above. Shooting stars soared past his head. Celestial bodies expanded and contracted. Selvig was in awe but unsure of his place in this new configuration. In the distance, a mysterious figure sat in a craggy chair atop a throne of boulders, facing out toward the cosmos.

"You are *shaken*, aren't you, old man?" Loki taunted. "Everyone was right about you. You're not well." He moved around Selvig, stalking him like prey. "Erik Selvig, you are a frightened animal, lying on the ground, unable to move. Not because you've been maimed, not because you've been bloodied, but because you are simply frightened by the forest. You know what it contains. The unknown creatures, waiting to attack you. I wouldn't get up and fight them, either, if I were you. I'd do exactly what you're doing: Lie there and pretend I was dead!"

Loki sent Selvig flying into a pile of gravel.

"HA-HA-HA!" The cosmos shook with laughter. The figure on the throne found this interaction to be amusing.

Selvig thrust himself out of the rubble and dusted

himself off. "I won't be controlled any longer," he growled.

FWASH!

A sphere of white light appeared, hovering above the ground in the distance. Its brightness pulsed like a heartbeat. Selvig heard it calling out to him in his head, comforting him. When he focused on the sphere, the stress of his current situation disappeared.

Loki shook his head. "You keep saying that, but I must admit, I still don't believe you," he said, tossing the Scepter in Selvig's direction.

"Yah!" Selvig said, ducking to avoid the blow. He looked past Loki to make sure the Scepter was gone, but it had already reappeared in Loki's hand.

"Magic," Loki said with a bow. "Or something *more*? You're the scientist. You tell me."

Selvig's strength started to build. "I *am* a scientist," he said. "It is my job to search for answers to the universe's impossible truths."

Loki yawned. "I've heard this monologue before."

"You'll hear it again, fiend," Selvig growled. "You

play games with humanity and leave us to clean up your messes. Take your toys and *go home*!"

FWASH!

The sphere's light grew brighter as the heavens above turned pitch-black. Loki shuddered at the sight. Selvig slowly moved toward the frightened god. They stared each other down, unblinking. "The hunter has become the hunted. How does that feel, Loki?" Selvig asked.

Loki did his best to appear unfazed. "I'm waiting to be impressed," he scoffed.

Selvig was, at last, face-to-face with his enemy. He felt calm. His thoughts were clear and collected. He delivered them plainly and without emotion. "You misused a great and powerful resource. You infected my world, and my mind, with galactic energies I barely understand. Because I didn't understand these energies, I feared them. I'm human, after all. But now I finally understand who's *really* in control of my fate. Me. I see that clearly now. And while my struggles may not be over, I refuse to play dead. Now give me my damn soul back!"

Selvig swiped the Scepter from Loki's grasp and tossed it, like a spear, into the great darkness that surrounded them.

"Good luck," Loki whispered, fading away.

The light of the white sphere ignited. The burst of energy blinded Selvig.

"HA-HA-HA!" The figure on the throne cackled again.

"I'm coming for you next," Selvig threatened.

———————

FWASH!

Suddenly, the planetoid was gone. Erik Selvig had awakened, safely, in Anoki's encampment. He was soaked in sweat.

"How was your nap?" Anoki asked, offering Selvig a cup of water. "Drink this. I swear there's nothing in it except good, old-fashioned hydration."

Selvig took the cup and drank. "I feel...good," he said. "Better." He sipped again. "What did I just experience?"

"It was a dream, Erik. Nothing more, nothing less. The things that appeared to you, whatever they might've been, were not real. They were represen-tations, manifestations of your struggles," Anoki explained. "Did you vanquish them?"

Selvig cracked a tiny smile. "I did," he said.

"Excellent. The healing process has been accel-erated. Your future is up to *you*." Anoki grinned. "Now leave me alone. I need to get back to a very important knitting project."

As Selvig and Darcy prepared to leave, Felix pulled Anoki aside. "Um, I hope this isn't weird or anything but, um, you know how you mentioned that Wakandan Outreach Centre?"

"I'd be happy to write you a letter of recommen-dation," Anoki said, handing Felix a business card. "Email me. *If* you survive your little expedition."

Felix felt energized but played it cool. "Right on," he said, bopping his head ever so slightly. "I'll email you. Soon. Not too soon, though. In, like, a week. Is that too soon?"

Anoki handed Selvig the invitation to Bixby's event. "Just in case."

Selvig inspected the note card. "This symbol," he

muttered, pointing to the half-moon. "What does it mean?"

"It's a crescent," Anoki said. "Bixby's new logo or some such."

"Thank you for this," Selvig said. "I hope to see you again soon, Anoki."

"Can we go home now *or no*?" Darcy asked.

Selvig looked to the sky. "There's been a change in plans."

CHAPTER 6

"Reverse Engineer!" Selvig shouted. "We come in peace."

Darcy looked out among the piles of garbage, wondering where she'd be if she hadn't answered Selvig's late-night call for help. "Tell me this is the last destination," she whined. "Please, please, please tell me we can go home after *this*."

They'd arrived at a junkyard in Compton, California. The property was surrounded by heaps of old tires, outdated electronics, furniture, and other assorted debris. In a corner, near the back of the property, was a tiny cottage owned by a man named Bisi Banyaga. To some in the scientific community, he was a legend. To others, he was a fraud. To his neighbors, he was a nuisance. Rumor on the street was that Banyaga was over one hundred years old. He'd started that rumor so people would tell him he looked younger. At six feet tall and three hundred pounds, Banyaga cut an imposing figure. He always wore the same thing: a "comfortably classic" red tracksuit. If you didn't know him, you might think he wanted to fight you until he flashed his million-dollar smile. In his early years, Banyaga studied engineering at the University of London, where he met Selvig. They bonded quickly over their love of science and their passion for knowledge. While Selvig went on to teach, Banyaga chose to make science his hobby, not his profession. He'd been courted by S.H.I.E.L.D. many times over but always declined their offers. It wasn't his style to do what people told him.

"I know you're here, Bisi. I can smell your cooking!" Selvig shouted.

Two enormous hounds descended from atop a pile of garbage two stories high. They bounded down, clumsily running up to Selvig, Darcy, and Felix, and stopping in front of them and staring in silence.

"Call off your pets, please?" Selvig asked. "I've serious business to discuss with you."

Banyaga opened the door to his cottage. "Is this about that interview in *Science Digest* where I called you a milquetoast bore, Erik?" he asked. "That was a joke!"

"No."

"Oh. Okay, then. Is it about Anjelica Tan's new boyfriend? I've only met him once. He's handsome, kind, a real sweetheart. Nothing like you; don't worry."

"What? She didn't tell me she had a new boyfriend," Selvig said. He didn't mean to get distracted. "That's *not* what I'm here to talk to you about today."

"What is it you want from me, then?" asked Banyaga. "Besides my good looks and stellar brain, that is."

"Help me save the world."

"Too broad!" Banyaga barked. "I'm very busy, but I'll consider it." He flipped a light switch inside his tiny house. And just like that, the hounds mysteriously vanished.

"Holograms," Selvig grumbled. "I should have been able to spot that."

"We all make mistakes, old man," Banyaga said. "Some more than others." He waved Selvig, Darcy, and Felix over, and they entered the cottage warily. It was sparsely decorated. Wires, circuits, and assorted technology sat in piles on the dinner table. A flat-screen TV played game shows on a loop. On the stove was a boiling pot of *Agatogo*, a flavorful Rwandan soup and one of Banyaga's favorites. "Sit there," he said, pointing to a love seat piled high with notebooks, magazine articles, and research.

As Felix cleared a spot, he scanned the curious documents, looking to see if any of them contained secrets. "Optogenetics? Why does that sound familiar?" he asked, flipping through an old, water-damaged notebook.

Banyaga swiped it from his hands. "That's not yours. Sit down and don't go through people's things," he scoffed. "Optogenetics is a technique that uses light to change the behavior of genetically modified tissues or organisms. One little flashbulb and BAM! Metamorphosis. Not exactly, but you know what I mean. A few years back, a group of local scientists were able to erase specific memories in laboratory mice. It left me fascinated. Oh, to be a human trial. There are more than a few painful childhood memories I'd love to burn to a crisp, but, alas, who has the time? We're the sum of all our parts—the good, the bad, and the ugly."

"Duuuuuude!" Felix moaned. "In the hands of the wrong person, that kind of genetic technology could be extremely dangerous. We're talking *mind wiping* here."

Banyaga was expressionless as he stared at Felix in silence.

"What?" asked Felix. "Why are you looking at me like that?"

Banyaga sighed. "Science, in all its forms, contains the building blocks of existence. It's inherently dangerous, no matter who uses it. Now, close your mouth and don't say another word, I'm going to guess Erik's plan." He rubbed his chin like a master detective, circling the room as he made his case.

"You're broken up about half the population kicking the bucket. Sleepless nights, restful days. Ran away from your problems as far as your spindly legs could take you. Then you heard about Iggy Bixby's sci-fi party. It burned your butt not to be invited. Now you're here, begging me to take you as my plus-one. Am I close?"

"Hardly," Selvig said. "I need to create a device that can harness cosmic energies and communicate directly with the collective consciousness of the universe."

"Oh cool. Something *easy*," Banyaga said, taking a seat at the table.

"Wait just a second," Darcy said. "I thought we were here to ask about Jane."

"The plan has changed," said Selvig.

"Jane! Love her. How's she doing?" Banyaga asked. The looks on their faces told him everything he needed to know. "Well, she's in a better place. Wherever that may be."

"She's not dead, Bisi," Selvig grumbled. "She's just—"

"Why did Doctor Selvig call you the Reverse Engineer?" Felix blurted out.

"Because that's what I do," Banyaga explained. "I take things apart, study them, and put them back together. Sometimes they work in new ways, and sometimes they don't. Everything is a work in progress."

Felix spotted a tribal mask on the wall. "What's that?" he asked, pointing.

"A dead alien head," said Banyaga. "Kidding. It's a piece of history. What's it to you? Writing a book?"

"Ahem!" Selvig dramatically pretended to clear his throat.

Banyaga glared at him from across the room. "I can definitely help you, Erik. Trust. But it'll cost you."

"These things always do," Selvig said. "What's the price?"

"I want to hear all about that juicy Tesseract," he purred. "The jewel of Odin's throne room! Haven't stopped thinking about that thing since I first read about it. Been a long time since you've visited me, so now that you're here, I want to hear your *firsthand* experiences. Oh, I need those hot S.H.I.E.L.D. secrets, Erik. I know you've got some that weren't in that big ol' info dump a few years back. Lay 'em on me!"

"You're *fun*," Darcy said. "Can we keep you?"

Banyaga giggled. "Girl, don't make me blush. You can't afford *all this*," he said, grandly presenting himself as if in front of a royal court. "Unless you know Captain America. For *him*, I'd travel far *and* wide. Add Bucky to the mix, and I'd definitely ship it."

"Sh-ship?" Selvig stuttered. "You'd ship...what?"

"Oh, Erik, you need to brush up on your Urban Dictionary," Banyaga said, shaking his head. "I don't have time to educate you on *everything*."

"Settle this for me, bigshot," Felix blurted out, raising his hand. "How did Captain America survive, trapped in a block of ice for, like, fifty years? That's impossible."

Banyaga cackled. "We've got gods and aliens

runnin' around our planet, and this kid wants to use the word *impossible*?! Steve Rogers was turned into a super-soldier, okay? *His body chemistry was changed.*"

"Yeah...b-but..." Felix stuttered.

"Mouth shut. Listen to your elders," Banyaga said. "There's this microorganism called a tardigrade, right? Ugly thing. I call it a *nightmare pig* cuz *that's what it looks like.* The tardigrade is quite special indeed. You see, it can metabolize glycogen in its liver, which then reduces the osmotic shrinkage of cells."

"Oh. Okay. I think I understand now. Cap's blood must've contained extreme amounts of glucose, which means the water in his blood was never able to freeze, which thereby preserved his body in the ice. Of course!" exclaimed Felix.

"Yes. *Of course. Now* he gets it," Banyaga said with a playful mocking tone. "The long and short of it is Captain America's enhanced blood contains a cryoprotectant, which allowed his body to remain in a state of icy hibernation. The man was, in a word, *preserved.*"

"Enough chatter," Selvig groused. "*Please*, Bisi. We came here with a purpose."

"I know, Erik!" Banyaga roared. "You need a device that can harness cosmic energies and communicate directly with the collective consciousness of the universe. *You already told me.* As if I'm just supposed to whip one up out of nowhere. *I could* if I had the resources."

Selvig tossed Bixby's party invitation onto the table.

"So, you got one," Banyaga said, inspecting the card. "Drone delivery?"

"Secondhand," replied Selvig. "If you tell me about Bixby's plan for the Crescent, I'm prepared to speak about the Tesseract."

"Bahp, bahp, bahp!" Felix exclaimed. "What's this Crescent business, now?"

"None of your concern, Felix. Stop questioning the mission," Selvig said. His frustration was showing. "Do we have a deal, Bisi?"

Banyaga quieted himself and adopted a sly poker face. "I'll put you on the path you need to be on,

Erik. Promise. Now...let's hear a little bit about that beautiful blue cube."

Selvig, having reached an agreement, settled in to tell the tale. "Tønsberg, Norway. March 1942," he said ominously.

"STOP! HOLD UP! NO!" Banyaga shouted. "Don't need to hear a history lesson, man. Certainly not *your* version. What I want are the details I can't get from a textbook or a S.H.I.E.L.D. info dump. I'd like to hear the Tesseract's *modern* journey, if you don't mind. Preferably the part where *its* story intertwines with *yours*, Erik."

Selvig recalibrated. "As you may know, after World War II, the Tesseract was recovered by Howard Stark. He moonlighted as one of the founding members of S.H.I.E.L.D., studying the device, but, sadly, he was never able to reignite its vast power supply. Decades later, director Nick Fury drafted me for Project P.E.G.A.S.U.S., which he'd been putting together at the Joint Dark Energy Mission Facility in the Mojave Desert. The project's goal was to crack the Tesseract's code, as it were. I surrounded myself with great minds. Superb think-ers. We worked very hard to deliver results, but even with S.H.I.E.L.D.'s resources, we couldn't break down the Tesseract's true origin. It was a cosmic item of power, yes, but it *had* to be rooted in science, as all things are. My team and I could get only so far in our research before we hit a brick wall. Then Loki arrived, and we were finally able to see the Tesseract's purpose realized. It was a gate-way through the universe."

Felix raised his hand. "Like a black hole?"

"No, no, no. Mass and energy cause curvatures in space-time, according to Einstein's Theory of Gen-eral Relativity. If the mass is extreme, these curva-tures can become so intense that light is unable to escape. *That's* a black hole. The Tesseract is differ-ent. It's a bridge, not a—"

"Hole."

"Correct. Theoretically, it's possible for the curva-ture to lean in the opposite orientation so it connects two different regions of space, creating a shortcut and allowing direct travel. One would need a negative mass to generate and stabilize a bridge so powerful, which is why this is merely a theory at the moment. It's unclear how the Tesseract produces this effect, but we do know its power can be amplified. Loki used his Scepter to enhance the Tesseract's power so much that it completely destroyed the Joint Dark Energy Mission Facility. He controlled my mind with that Scepter. He made me do terrible things." Selvig tried his best not to get emotional as he recalled the events, but he wasn't having much luck. "Imagine being caged inside your own body. That's what I experienced while under his influence. Loki had me create a device that focused the Tesseract's energy to open a portal that brought an army of barbaric extraterrestrials to our planet. The Chitauri laid waste to New York City because of conditions *I* created while under Loki's influence. I think about that. Every day."

Felix put his hand on Selvig's shoulder, speaking softly. "Don't go there, Doc."

"My cousin found a Chitauri behind a dumpster in Queens a few years ago. The thing was eating rats and crying. Or so she said," Banyaga claimed.

"That's impossible. The Chitauri hive mind got shut down during the Battle of New York. There's no way one of them was still up and running," said Felix.

"Well, my cousin *is* also a *known* liar," Banyaga said. "Erik, your story is captivating if incomplete. Where's the Tesseract now, and would you be willing to take me there?"

"Thor took the Tesseract back to Asgard where, I assume, it still lives," Selvig said, exhaling. "I believe you now have a promise to keep, Bisi. What is Bixby planning? What do you know about the Crescent?"

Banyaga leaned back in his chair. "I don't know what this Crescent is that you speak of."

Selvig pointed at the invitation. "The symbol. The half-moon. The Crescent."

"Oh that? It's called branding," Banyaga said. "You know who can answer your question a lot better than I can? *Bixby*." He took a deep breath. "Our agreement was for me to put you on the path you need to be on, so that's what I'm going to do. Go to Ignatius Bixby's party. That's the path. End of story."

"Absolutely not!" Selvig exclaimed. "I won't entertain the thought."

"You want the truth? Bixby's been stockpiling materials. Elements. Metals. There have been *rumors*. I wasn't going to tell you this because it's all just gossip, which you know I love, but I don't trust it. Then I looked at the patterns and...Bixby is definitely up to something. Usually, he's all over the place, showing off whatever junky thing he's made, talking, talking, talking. But not this time. That loudmouth has gone totally *silent*. When I got the invite to his party, that's when I knew. He's got a trick up his sleeve. He's about to play his hand. According to the patterns, he may have whatever this thing is that you want. Go, don't go, makes no difference to me, but the party's happening, so you'll need to make a decision pretty quick."

Darcy sighed. "How far away is this thing?" she asked. "Please don't tell me it's in another state. My poor car is on her last legs."

"You're in luck. It's thirty minutes away. How's that for a cosmic coincidence?" Banyaga asked.

"Traffic should be light." He whipped a knapsack off a shelf and tossed it at Selvig. "You're gonna need what's in that if you want this operation to remain covert. Ask Darcy to help you figure out a look."

Selvig peeked into the bag. "This is filled with wigs," he said, perplexed.

"Yes, and they're expensive, too. I want them, back," Banyaga said. "Now, get out of here. I need to eat my *Agatogo* and watch my stories."

Darcy was exhausted. Felix ached for excitement. Selvig wasn't sure what to do next. He felt backed into a corner. He knew Banyaga wouldn't steer him into a trap, but the last thing he wanted to do was attend Bixby's gathering. It was written all over his face.

"Don't get in the way of yourself, Erik. You'll trip," Banyaga said. He thought about his words for a moment. "Should I put that on a T-shirt? I should put that on a T-shirt."

The wheels turned inside Selvig's head. Time was running out.

CHAPTER 7

"This is it. This is the end," Darcy sniffled. "After
all these years, it's time to finally say good-bye." She
lay dramatically across the hood of the *Mary Jackson*,
petting her car as if it were a family pet being laid
to rest. "You were valiant till the end, girl. Rest in
peace." The short drive from Bisi Banyaga's junkyard in
Compton to Ignatius Bixby's compound in the Hollywood Hills was too much for Darcy's car to bear.
After countless road trips, errands, late-night snack
runs, and impromptu beach excursions, the *Mary
Jackson* rolled to a stop and died. Selvig was anxious
for Darcy's episode to end.

"Enough, Darcy," he said. "Let's get going."

"This car was my life, Erik. I was living in it
when Jane hired me. It's the only thing I've ever

owned if you don't count my college debt." Darcy drew a smiley face in the soot that covered the driver's side window. She kissed the roof of the dirty car and bid adieu. "Ya ain't much to look at but ya gave me a lot of good years. I'm gonna miss you, girl."

"I'm really sorry, Darcy," Felix said. He put his hand on her shoulder as a comforting gesture. "She stank like Cheez Doodles and gasoline, but I'll never forget her. Rest in peace."

"We're losing time," groaned Selvig. "Bixby's expo is getting underway." He threw up his hands in a manic panic. "It was just *a car.*"

Darcy had reached her wit's end. "*Just a car* that wouldn't have died had it not driven cross-country on *your quest*!" she snapped.

Selvig made a pithy noise. "New Mexico to California is hardly cross-country."

"I'm *done*," Darcy said. She popped the trunk, grabbed her backpack, and started walking.

"We've reached our destination," Selvig said. "Stop being so emotional."

The sheer rudeness stopped Darcy in her tracks.

"Excuse me, *Selvig*. Do you know how many times I've shown up for you? Because I do. I show up. *A lot*. I take you everywhere you want to go. I've spent nights doing your filing. I've spent mornings cataloging your reports. I've missed birthdays, bar mitzvahs, my landlady's funeral. Oh, and I've almost been killed by aliens and a..."

"Jotunheim beast," reminded Felix.

"Yeah, one of those!" Darcy said, shaking her finger in the air. Her tone turned serious. "I believe in you, Erik. I love science. I respect the truth. But this wild-goose chase you've taken us on has exhausted me, and I need some space, like, *now*." She took off down the street, walking briskly and trying not to think about where she was going.

Felix ran to Darcy and made a final appeal to keep her from leaving. "Come inside. *Please*. We came all this way. We're so close to..." He wasn't sure what to say. "We're close to *something*. Okay? We *have* to be. Let's just go inside, check it out, and then you can walk away from this gig forever. I know I'm just some smart-ass kid who came along for the ride, but up that hill is a party, and I'm wearing a bow tie. If that's not fate, I don't know what is." Felix's lame joke made Darcy giggle. "We can't do this without you."

"I beg your pardon?" Selvig said.

"All your science buddies knew it! Why don't you? It takes a village, man. Darcy is the glue that's keeping our little village together," Felix replied. "Why are you serving us all this attitude, Doc? I thought your mind was healed."

Selvig undid a few buttons on his shirt. He needed the air. "Ignatius Bixby has been a thorn in my side for a very long time. The thought of confronting him makes me nervous." He took a seat on the curb. "The man has been badgering me to join him for ages. He's thrown money at me repeatedly, but it always came with *strings*. I learned to ignore him. Eventually, he stopped. Men like him make me seethe. Con men, opportunists who build their names on the backs of hardworking people."

"Does *he* know what *we* know about the Tesseract and the Aether?" Felix asked.

"I assume so, based on what Bisi told us. Bixby is a despicable human being. If he's built something that can harness their power…if he now possesses a device that can communicate with forces beyond what we know…" There was fear in Selvig's eyes. "It's the end."

"Doc, there was this one night, when you first came to the hotel," Felix began. "I heard you in your room, talking to yourself, going through all this *knowledge*, lining up all these things that sounded awesome. Then you got really mad. Started banging on your desk. Something about how you couldn't go back. You got so bent out of shape over the Water of Sight. Then I never heard you mention it again. Why is that?"

"Felix, you don't understand what you're talking about," Selvig said. He stood up from the curb. "I won't discuss it any further."

"What if Bixby can actually *help us*? The guy has resources. So, what if there are strings attached? We'll just use him for what we need and cut him off when all is said and done. All options should be on the table," Felix said. "What if the Water of Sight is the key that unlocks everything? He could help us figure out—"

"The Water of Sight is far too dangerous for human beings to tamper with. I've seen its power firsthand. Thor could barely handle the experience. It's unpredictable. An unknown quantity. It can't be controlled, which means it can't be studied, which means it's of no use to my work," Selvig said."

Felix shook his head in frustration. "*Blah, blah, blah*. You're afraid. Just admit it and walk away. Where's the Doctor Selvig who pushes boundaries and goes the distance when the odds are stacked against him, huh? I thought you were better than this, dude."

"I won't be lectured to by a child, prodigy or not!" Selvig bellowed.

SWACK!

Darcy tossed the wig bag, bopping Selvig in the face.

"Put a wig on, and shut your pie hole. *Both of you*," she snapped. "We're wasting time out here jibber-jabbering."

Selvig pulled out a wig made of long brown hair that was ratty and tangled. He felt around inside the bag for something to complete his disguise and came across two pieces of a goatee. He stuck them on his face and smiled like a goon. "I look ridiculous."

"Not bad for a secret agent on a budget," Darcy said. She placed a wig full of bouncing blonde locks atop her head and mugged for an imaginary camera.

Felix searched the bag, but there was nothing left for him to wear. "Um, what about my disguise?!" he said. "I'm part of this op, too."

"You're not a world's most famous scientist," Darcy said. "You'll be fine."

Selvig was miserable in his getup. His head itched. His face itched. He looked like a fool. None of that mattered. He was here now, and it was time to execute the mission.

"What's the plan, Doc?" asked Felix.

Selvig remained quiet. He was lost in thought.

"We'll feel things out, get a sense of the room," Darcy said. "Leave the aliases to me."

Felix, Darcy, and Selvig trudged up the steep driveway to find Bixby's hillside compound quiet and unguarded. As events went, this one looked fairly tame from the outside. No mingling on the terrace. No pool-party antics. As the trio approached the sprawling estate, they heard the faint sound of music coming from inside. The front door opened automatically, welcoming them to Bixby-Con. Inventors, pseudo-scientists, infomercial salespeople, and internet celebrities had set up booth displays around the perimeter of the home, each one showcasing some seemingly incredible breakthrough. VR experiences, craft tables, and demonstrations abounded.

Selvig scanned the room, looking for familiar faces, but didn't find a single one. "These people are all fakes, quacks, and reality television stars," he said nervously.

"Take it easy. We just got here," Darcy said. "It's an oddball science fair, not the grand expo we imagined. Who cares? We're not here for anyone but Bixby. Stay focused."

A cater waiter shoved a tray of meatballs in Selvig's face. "Care for a Pym Particle?" he asked. "They're filled with ricotta cheese."

"*Yes!*" Felix shouted. He popped three into his mouth and gobbled them up quickly.

"Thank you," Selvig said reluctantly, taking a meatball from the tray. He bit into it and winced.

A cheerful woman was positioned at a table in the foyer, checking in guests as they arrived. She wore a large white name tag that said LINDA ♥. In front of her, spread out across the table, were hundreds of unclaimed name tags.

"Hello, hello, hello!" Linda said. "Welcome to the first annual Bixby-Con! *Yay!*" She whipped out a clipboard from under the table, clearly anxious to cross off a name. "Who might you be?"

"I'll tell you in just one second, Linda." Darcy carefully scanned the assemblage of name tags. Some were foreign while others were strikingly familiar. "Cho, Halliwell, Benhamou, Marlow…Banner?! *These* people aren't coming here. Are they?!"

Linda was embarrassed by the question. "Mr.

Bixby arranged the table. Some of them are just for show, I guess," she admitted. "What do *I* know? I found this job on the internet. Ha-ha!"

"Been there, girl," Darcy said. She looked through the name tags some more. "A lot of fame hogs and filler biddies. A couple of legit science folk, too, I see."

Linda jiggled her clipboard. "And what category might *you* fall into?"

Darcy selected a name tag and showed it off for all to see. "Penny Miller, Microneural Biologist at your service!" She grabbed another name tag and pinned it on Selvig. "And my good pal Brizan Versteeg, Renewable Energy Developer."

"Thank you, Penny," Selvig said flatly.

Felix nudged Darcy in the ribs. *"Where's mine, Penny?"*

Darcy took a blank name tag, wrote *Felix, Intern* in big red letters, and slapped it on his chest.

Selvig patted his pockets. "Linda, I seem to have lost my itinerary."

"Not a problem," Linda replied. She handed him

a pamphlet that said BIXBY-CON in big, bold letters and featured a photograph of Ignatius Bixby's head where the O should be. His face was round and orange from years of bad tanning experiences. Bixby's eyes bulged, and his teeth sat millimeters apart from one another. He looked as if he were about to burst. Linda opened the pamphlet and gave her verbal tour. "Here's everything you need to know. There's a map of the floor and a schedule of events. Highlights include Biomisting, Smart Blobs, and I highly recommend you check out Doctor Elodie's Entropic Circuit. This evening Anna & the Ablations will be performing many of their hits, including 'Vaporize,' which is my favorite. Bathrooms are on the ground floor. Refreshment stations are located throughout the premises. Don't forget to have your photo taken with the Vysion!"

"Say what?" Darcy said. "*Uhhh*, that name is off-limits."

"Oh no. This is spelled with a *Y*," clarified Linda.

"V-I-S-Y-O-N?"

"No, V-Y-S-I-O-N."

"Well, that's just dumb," Darcy declared.

"Don't look at *me*, *I* didn't build it," said Linda. "Mr. Bixby will be making an announcement shortly from the balcony. Do *not* go upstairs. That area is *off-limits*. Oh, and keep your hands off the Permeable Membrane. I think that covers everything."

"You've been incredibly helpful, Linda," Darcy said. "Thank you."

Linda was pleased to be of service. "No problem. I'm really putting my political science degree to good use, huh? Ha-ha-ha-ha. Have fun, you guys!"

"These people are losers," Felix mumbled.

"*We're* here. What does that make us?" asked Darcy.

Felix thought for a moment. "Aspirational winners."

"It's no wonder that Bisi, Anjelica, and Anoki wouldn't be caught dead here. These people are all shams. They're not real scientists; they're wannabe celebrities. Fame, not the betterment of humanity, seems to be driving their choices," Selvig intoned.

"We're not here for them. We're here for Bixby.

Stay the course, Doc. Answers are coming our way. I can feel it," Felix said. "And, um, I might need to pee."

"At last!" Selvig said. He'd spotted someone he knew and tried to get their attention. "Doctor Mansoor Amjed! Amjed, old friend! Over here!"

Darcy yanked him by the arm. "You're not Erik Selvig right now. Remember? This is not the time to play catch-up with your pals," she warned. "Also, mask your accent or, better yet, don't talk to anybody."

Selvig removed Darcy's hand. "There's no need to handle me like a child," he said, straightening his shirt. "If I'm to *be* Brizan Versteeg, then I'll commit to the part." In an instant, Selvig had disappeared into the crowd.

"I really hope we don't get killed today." Darcy sighed. "Felix, *Linda* was a political science major *just like me*. Does that mean *this* is my future? This is probably the wrong time to have an identity crisis but..." She turned to find Felix had disappeared.

He'd meandered over to a booth covered in twinkling Christmas lights, where a woman dressed in a red tuxedo made of lamé fabric was quietly dozing off. Behind her were fifty small cages containing fifty small bunny rabbits and a sign that said SCIENTIFICA'S MIRACULOUS GENE DRIVES. Felix whistled, waking her up. The startled woman scrambled to cover.

"Hello, young sir!" Scientifica said. She shook out her arms and legs while making odd facial expressions. "Sorry about that. You caught me meditating. Welcome to Scientifica's Miraculous Gene Drives. I'm your hostess, Sci—"

Felix cut her off. "Save the razzle-dazzle, lady. What's this all about?"

"*Direct.* I like that," Scientifica said. "What I'm offering the scientific community is true innovation. A technology that creates a unique genetic trait and inserts it directly into an organism. These traits, known as Gene Drives, would then modify the DNA of that organism, eventually spreading through the population."

"And the bunnies?"

"All the rabbits you see behind me have experienced a Gene Drive. Their digestive systems were modified, allowing them to eat meat instead of vegetables."

Darcy tapped Felix on the shoulder. "I'm sure you find this riveting, but we need to move on," she said. They nodded kindly at Scientifica and drifted into the crowd.

"Hurry back," Scientifica yawned, returning to her nap.

Selvig floated through the room, snooping on conversations, asking strangers about what brought them to the event. Most of them were crowd fillers, hired by Bixby to mingle and have a good time. Selvig despised having to interact with these people, but he had to do it if he wanted to find out the truth. A peculiar fellow wearing a name tag that said Daryll bellied up to the refreshment stand where Selvig had perched himself. Daryll was an average guy with brown hair and a medium build. He eyed the room like a hawk before settling on Selvig.

"Excuse me, but has anyone ever talked to you about Quantum Futurism?" he asked.

"Not interested," murmured Selvig.

"I'd love to chat with you sometime about the Lennox theory," Daryll said.

"No, thank you," Selvig said. His tone grew harsher.

"If you'd prefer, we can discuss the effects of the Gaudet-Bowie Law of—"

Selvig had heard enough. "Stop your cult-y, faux-scientific claptrap," he said. "Please leave me alone. I'm here on real business."

"Oh! You should have said that first. I thought you were one of the actors, so I gave you my pyramid scheme spiel," Daryll said. He took a swig of soda. "I hear Bixby is debuting something big that's gonna change everything."

"He's a vampire. Buying up technology, cannibalizing other people's discoveries and claiming them as his own."

"But ... *you're* here," Daryll said.

"I'm out of options and, I'm ashamed to say, a little desperate." Before Selvig could ask him about

Bixby's announcement, a recognizable voice whispered in his ear.

"A little desperation never hurt anybody." Selvig turned to find himself face-to-face with the man of the hour—Ignatius Bixby. He was a short man in a tight black T-shirt and tan slacks. His thick white hair was slicked back, and, from afar, it looked as if he were wearing a helmet. Though wealthy, Bixby lacked a sense of style. He didn't care about that in the slightest. "I don't believe we've met." He eyed Selvig's name tag curiously. "Brizan Versteeg and I own a yacht together. The *Scientific American*. You're not him."

Selvig remembered Darcy's warning. He quickly cleared his throat and dropped his Norwegian accent. "Ahem! Oh dear. I must have selected the wrong tag. My apologies."

"It happens. Are you enjoying yourself, whoever you are?"

Selvig barely mustered a smile. "Absolutely."

"Lot of quacks at this thing, right? I tried to get the big guns, but you know how it goes with scheduling. They'll all wish they had come once I whip out *my* big gun."

Now Selvig's interest was doubly piqued. He hated being so close to Bixby but knew that this was his chance to get crucial information. "Do tell," he said.

"Nah. You'll be blown away soon enough. Ha-ha-ha." Bixby chuckled. "Gotta go get ready." He slapped Selvig on the back and took off upstairs. The unveiling was about to begin.

Elsewhere, Darcy and Felix strolled through the event, looking over each exhibitor's table. They had their eyes peeled for trouble, though neither of them knew what it looked like. A video presentation caught their attention at an unmanned booth in the middle of the room.

"Smart Blobs! The future of fun is *now*!" the video began. On screen, two tired-looking children tossed balls of spotted slime at each other while a strange woman watched from nearby. "Each gelatinous ball is filled with hundreds of tiny robotic nanites designed to keep your family entertained for minutes!"

"This is some gimmicky fake-science trash," Felix murmured. He motioned to the barrel of lime-green Smart Blobs. They looked as if they were in the process of melting into one another. "Take one, Darcy," he nudged. "They're free."

Darcy was uninterested. "No, thanks." In the distance, she spotted a woman dressed casually in a simple jacket and jeans. She had her hair pulled back into a ponytail and was wearing a baseball cap sporting the logo for Culver University. The woman moved through the room with careful consideration, though that wasn't the thing that caught Darcy's attention. There was a hole in the cap, slight but present.

That looks like my hat, Darcy thought, moving to get a better look. *The one I loaned to Jane.*

CHAPTER 8

Darcy slipped through the crowd, ducking and weaving around the attendees in an attempt to reach the woman before she slipped away.

A cater waiter thrust a tray of drinks in Darcy's face. "Gamma Bomb?"

"No, thanks," she said, pushing the tray away and continuing toward the woman.

The closer Darcy got, the more confident she became. *It has to be her*, she thought. *That's my hat*. Finally, she'd navigated her way across the room, stepping in the woman's way and blocking her from moving. "Jane?" Darcy said, standing eye to eye.

Doctor Jane Foster was shocked and confused. She never expected to see Darcy under these circumstances. She didn't expect to see anyone she knew at this particular event. It was part of the reason she felt comfortable attending. Jane, overwhelmed by the moment, pulled Darcy through a set of curtains and into an alcove. "Darcy, what are you doing here? And why are you wearing a Dolly wig?"

Darcy grabbed Jane and hugged her tightly. "You have no idea how good it is to see you right now. No idea. Jane, we thought you might be—"

Jane pulled out of the hug. "Don't," she said, placing her finger on Darcy's lips. "I'm here. I'm alive. And everything is going to be okay." She looked around, expecting someone else to join them. "You're here with Erik?"

"He's here, checking things out. It's been an interesting couple of days, to say the least," Darcy said. "Should I wait to ask you a million questions? Because I have a million questions. The first and most important one being—*where have you been?!*"

Jane nervously paced around the small area. She had come to the event with a plan in place but seeing Darcy changed all that. Jane took a seat on a nearby chair and gazed at Darcy's face. It was comforting to see her after being alone for so long. "I had to take myself off the grid," Jane said. "To protect you. To protect Erik. To protect my work. There are forces out there, Darcy. Unbelievably powerful forces of chaos and destruction. They defy what we know about the natural world. The Tesseract...the Aether...those were just the beginning."

"Now you're sounding like Erik," Darcy said. "He was doing great until the decimation made his head all clouded again."

"I figured as much. I'm sorry I haven't been around to help steer him back on the right path, but there are things I know that he doesn't. Things I kept from him because I thought they might send him over the edge." Jane exhaled. "I hope it's not too late."

Suddenly, Felix burst through the curtains. "Darcy, don't leave me like that again! Some weirdo tried to get me to—" Felix noticed Jane. "Oh. Em. Gee." He shook his head as if he couldn't believe what he was seeing. When he opened his mouth, the words poured out a mile a minute. "Doctor Foster, you are legit one of my all-time heroes. Not that I have a poster of you or anything. I would if I had a room. Or a house for that matter. I'm kind of homeless. Whatever. Doesn't matter. Your work is totally inspiring. The Einstein-Rosen bridge is the reason I'm obsessed with science. Well, one of the reasons. My parents are scientists. *Were* scientists. They're not physically on this plane of existence any longer, but I can feel them with me. Conservation of energy and all that. You feel me. I just have to say, Doctor Foster, you've been such an influence in my life and not just scientifically speaking. I also enjoy creative writing. Would you be open to reading my wormhole fanfic? You don't have to answer. Just think about it. Oh man, to know it's possible to open a gateway to another world...It changed my whole outlook on life. Thank you for that. You're honestly the best."

Jane looked at Darcy. "Friend of yours?" she asked.

"This is Felix," replied Darcy.

"I'm the new intern," Felix said, pointing to his name tag. He fished the Bixby-Con pamphlet out of his pocket and offered it to Jane. "Would you mind signing this?"

"Not *now*, dude," said Darcy.

"It's great to meet you, Felix. I appreciate your kind words," Jane said.

Felix rubbed his hands together anxiously. "Can I get you a Pym Particle? Or maybe a Gamma Bomb? I think I saw some shrimp on a tray. I could get you some of those?"

"No, thank you," Jane said. "We need to find Erik. It's time I told him everything."

An announcement blared over a PA system. "Please make your way to the main area. Mr. Bixby will be speaking momentarily."

Darcy felt uneasy. "What's about to go down, Jane?" she asked. "And have you talked to Thor lately? He has my Bill Nye DVDs. I want them back."

"I'm going to go ahead and say that those DVDs are probably gone," Jane replied.

Felix poked his head through the curtain and spotted Selvig on the other side of the room, munching on hors d'oeuvres. He caught his eye and energetically waved him over.

"This is gonna be *weird*," Darcy said.

Selvig flung open the curtains and entered the alcove. Selvig and Jane embraced warmly and in silence. He stared at her smiling face for a moment, taking it in, processing the moment. "When your father passed years ago, I took it upon myself to make sure I was always present should you ever need my counsel. Protecting you was my responsibility, and I took it very seriously. So, know I ask this with compassion, from a place of love—Jane, where the devil have you *been*?! You took off without saying a word. If you needed space, so be it, but why didn't you tell anyone where you were going?! Why didn't you come forward after the decimation to let us know you were at least safe?"

"I owe you a full explanation, Erik. I'm sorry it hasn't happened sooner," Jane began. "It was never my intention to mislead you. Please believe me when I say that. My work led me in a direction that I didn't plan on going. Involving you and Darcy meant putting you in danger, and I couldn't do that. I had to go it alone. To be honest, I didn't plan on even being here today, but I believe Bixby may be up to something, and I needed to know for sure."

Selvig nodded. He didn't fully understand Jane's perspective, but he respected her tremendously and accepted her response. She was one of the greatest minds on the planet. She knew what she was doing. "Then let us compare notes," Selvig said.

"I'm getting the chills right now," Felix said. "Anyone else?"

Selvig went full steam ahead. "The decimation event is tied to the items of power we've come into contact with, Jane. They have a very specific energy. You and I have felt it firsthand. It's left a residue inside us," he explained. "I needed to know more about your experience with the Aether, so Darcy, Felix, and I set out to find you. While Anjelica Tan was unable to direct us to your whereabouts, she gave me access to your video journals. You mentioned a book on Asgard that spoke of items that had the power to control the universe. Is that what you've been investigating?"

"Yes," Jane said. "But how did you ... ?"

"I hacked the encryption," Felix said with an embarrassed shrug. "Sorry."

"While I was being kept on Asgard, I happened upon Odin's library. I wasn't supposed to go in there, but I did. What else was I supposed to do? I had a lot of time to kill. There was one book in particular. I thought it was fiction. The story sounded so insane. Colorful stones made up of raw cosmic energy, each one imbued with unique powers. I mean, that sounds made-up, right?"

"Said the ex-girlfriend of a god," Darcy whispered. Felix gently elbowed her in the side.

"I'd forgotten about the book. My experience with the Aether had consumed me completely. It wasn't until I had some distance that I realized what I'd read. It wasn't just a story, it was the truth. As the healing process continued, the memories came flooding back. The Aether, the Tesseract, Loki's Scepter... they're all connected, Erik. You're absolutely right. You and I have come into contact with the most powerful forces in existence: the Infinity Stones."

Selvig was relieved to hear his mania hadn't been

in vain. He was desperate for more information. "Go on...."

"The six Infinity Stones were born at the beginning of the universe. Each one represents a unique aspect of the universe: time, space, mind, reality, power, and soul. The stones were far too powerful. So, in order to contain them, each one was placed into a protective casing that would temper its abilities and make it difficult to locate."

Selvig was mesmerized by the revelation. "The Tesseract...it's...it's just a casing for..."

"The Space Stone. It creates gateways, Einstein-Rosen bridges, though on a completely different scale. Its wielder can open portals and teleport across vast distances. Nothing is off-limits. No place in the universe is inaccessible. The Space Stone is also an incredible energy source that can be used to power virtually anything."

"Its power is so great that the only way it can be contained and controlled is by placing it in an encapsulation shell," said Felix. "In the Tesseract's case, a blue cube."

"Yes!" Jane exclaimed. "That's it exactly."

Darcy didn't understand. "But the Aether isn't a stone . . . it's like a . . . blood cloud?"

"Correct. And there's a reason for that. The Aether is the Reality Stone," Jane revealed. "While it was inside me, I experienced only a fraction of its abilities. Its shapeless form can possess a host body and give the body unlimited strength and unpredictable power. We knew that. But in its solid form, it can create illusions and twist our perceptions."

"Then it *is* a Radical Quantum Selector!" Felix exclaimed. "Hugh Everett III, the super-famous physicist, proposed that there are an infinite number of parallel universes out there. A lot of them would be similar to our own, while others could be totally different. Simply put, any reality you can think of? It exists. Sounds to me as if the Aether functions like a Radical Quantum Selector that allows its wielder to access these alternate realities and manifest them into our physical universe. Am I close?"

Jane was impressed. "You're *good*."

"Indeed, he is," Selvig said. "Continue, please."

"The purple Power Stone has the ability to destroy worlds. Whole. Its casing is known as the Orb. The green Time Stone allows its wielder to go backward or forward in time, changing whatever they see fit," Jane explained. "Erik, you mentioned Loki's Scepter and you're right. It factors into all this as well. The Scepter was merely the thing that housed the yellow Mind Stone, capable of controlling thoughts and actions. Once all the Stones have been assembled, the wearer could control the totality of existence," said Jane. "The Stones could be on Earth right this very moment. I believe the decimation event was triggered by the Stones working in concert."

"You said there were six stones," Felix said, "but you mentioned only five."

"The orange Soul Stone is the mystery of the bunch. Its power is unconfirmed as are its whereabouts," Jane said. "At first, I thought Bixby might actually *have* one of the Stones, but then I intercepted a communication that...scared me. I know you think Bixby is a fool, and there's truth to that, but you need to understand the stakes here—if *you're* involved in something he wants to be involved in it, too. I've been keeping tabs on him, and he's been keeping tabs on you. Now he's built some kind of device he's going to use to destroy the planet."

"No," Selvig said. "That's not what the Crescent was meant to—" Selvig bit his lip. "One night as I lay in bed in that dank motel room, restless, exhausted, a concept came to me. One of many that ate at my once-clouded brain. I forgot about it, wrote it off, until I saw the symbol on Anoki's invitation."

"Wait a minute," Darcy said. "That half-moon you scribbled on your wall was the same symbol from the invitation? And it's a device?"

"Bixby has somehow co-opted my idea....He's mocking me...."

Jane looked Selvig in the eye. "What does the Crescent *do*, Erik?"

Suddenly, the lights dimmed, and the crowd quieted. Bixby was about to make his grand entrance.

CHAPTER 9

"Ladies, gentlemen, scientists of all disciplines,
the time has come for you to silence your phones.
The main event is upon us! You'll not want to miss
out!" A voice that sounded strikingly like Bixby's
boomed over the intercom. "Seriously, make sure
your phones are turned off." There were ten seconds
of silence while the crowd collectively checked their
phones. "All right! You know him as the inventor of
the Handi-Pan. You know him as a television personality who's appeared on shows like *Doodad King* and
What IS That? He has over five hundred thousand
followers who are definitely *not bots*. Please put your
hands together for the one, the only, the self-taught,
Ignaaaaaatius BIXBY!"

The lights turned on as the man of the hour

emerged from behind a velveteen red curtain. Applause erupted like a volcano of sound. The assembled super-science wannabes couldn't get enough.

"Pathetic," muttered Selvig.

Bixby soaked it all up. He closed his eyes and thrust his fist into the air as if he'd just won the lottery. "You spoil me," he said, adjusting his microphone headset. As the applause died down, Bixby strolled around the balcony, working himself into an emotional lather. "Look at the person next to you. *Do it.*" The crowd followed the order. "One day soon the person you're looking at is going to be *someone*. They may be an unimportant nobody *now*. Your peers may consider you a *joke* or 'not a real scientist.' Are they right?"

After an awkward pause, the crowd released a series of angry, insecure boos.

"Exactly! Because you *are* real scientists!" Bixby shouted. The room filled with cheers and applause yet again. The master of ceremonies was pleased.

"Ugh. This is so gross," Darcy complained.

"You're never gonna believe this, but I was like

you once—a complete nothing," Bixby said, sauntering around his space. "I wanted success so bad I could taste it. All I had was failure, and guess what? It didn't taste good!" He pantomimed spitting. The crowd tittered. "I did what I had to do to survive. I learned to take other people's work and elevate it—"

"*Stole*," growled Selvig. "He *stole* other people's work."

"And now I'm rich. You do the math," Bixby said with a shrug. The crowd withheld their applause. He remained unfazed. "Our planet recently experienced a great catastrophe. I was in my hot tub when it happened. My poor assistants, Kaitlyn and Connor, disintegrated into the water right in front of me. It was terrible. I had to drain the tub, disinfect the whole thing. I couldn't use it for weeks." He stopped to sniffle. "And my assistants were gone." His sad tone soon replaced with anger. "That day I vowed to get to the bottom of the decimation event. What my research soon uncovered was shocking. We think of the Avengers as *heroes*, but have you ever noticed how *they're* the ones who attract unsavory elements from beyond the stars? Aliens, robots, other assorted phenomena. These things didn't exist until people like Captain America showed up. Love him, btw, but c'mon. Tony Stark?! Who does he think he is?! These people sickened our planet with cosmic power when their battles ended and the dust settled; these cosmic energies didn't *evaporate*. They seeped into our cities, our lands." He paused for effect. "And maybe even our bodies. Who's to say? But the fact remains—our world is littered with celestial forces whether we like it or not. Think of them as *cosmic backwash*." The crowd erupted with laughter.

"That's *my* line," growled Darcy. *"He stole my line."*

"That's what he does," Selvig muttered.

"We must not be controlled by these forces! It's time to fight!" Bixby cheered. An assistant wheeled out a pedestal upon which a mystery item sat covered by shimmering black cloth with detailed gold fringe. "It's time to get our *souls* back."

Bixby stared at the audience, smiling. He flicked his tongue. "You guys wanna see what's underneath?"

"YEAH!" Now the audience was frothing at the mouth.

Bixby whipped off the cloth to reveal a sleek silver device. It was the size of a Frisbee and curved, resembling a half-moon. There was a tiny, open control panel on its underside.

"There it is…" Felix gasped.

"This, my friends, is the *Crescent*. My greatest invention. It serves as a conduit of cosmic energy that will allow humanity to access the heavens themselves." He circled the pedestal, presenting the device for all to see. "We will no longer be pawns in the universe's sick games. Earth shall be reclaimed by *humanity*!"

Selvig was incensed.

"We gotta steal that thing out from under him," Felix said, bursting at the seams. "Hear me out, okay? If it's a conduit of cosmic energy, wouldn't we be able to use it to jump-start the Water of Sight? I know I'm not supposed to bring that place up, but deal with it. Since the Water of Sight is supposed to be, like, a window into the universe, or whatever, why can't we get those Gravimetric Spikes you used during the Convergence and use them in conjunction with the Crescent to stabilize the event? That would work, right? In theory. I mean, we could blow this whole Infinity Stones thing wide open." Felix rubbed his forehead. "My brain hurts."

Selvig was quiet, lost in thought. Felix's idea made sense, but executing such a thing wouldn't be easy. It would require a detailed plan as well as considerable time and effort. At the moment, they didn't have any of those things. *"Þat sem ek óttask geymir þat sem ek þarfask,"* Selvig said. "The thing I *fear* contains the thing I *need*," he whispered. "Felix is right. Now that we know the vast cosmic scope of our mission, it's time to face the music. We've got to steal the Crescent and get to the Water of Sight before Bixby gets there first."

"Say what now?" Darcy asked.

"Felix saw the bigger picture, and now so do I," Selvig said. He turned to Jane for guidance. He wasn't about to embark on this mission without her. "Can we do this?"

"Can we accomplish the task of activating the

Water of Sight using *that* device?" Jane asked. "Maybe. My knowledge of the Water of Sight isn't much outside of a passing mention, but I'll be able to figure it out. I'd obviously need my equipment."

"We'll get everything we need," Selvig said. "Right now is our only chance to retrieve the Crescent. We must take it."

"*This is crazy talk*," Darcy pressed. "We are not these people!"

Selvig was undeterred. "Jane, you'll need to sneak upstairs and snatch the Crescent on my signal. Darcy, Felix, you'll have to create a distraction once Jane has the device." He placed his hand on Darcy's shoulder. "Thank you for never giving up on me. I need you. Now more than ever. Are you with me?"

"Of course. I can't say *no now*. Then *I'd* be the jerk," Darcy said. "What are *you* gonna do?"

Selvig stood up. He ripped off his goatee and wig and tossed them into the crowd. "I'm going to give Bixby what he wants."

Felix's eyes widened. "It. Is. *On*." He and Darcy slipped away to get into their positions.

"Ignatius!" Selvig yelled. "What do you think you're doing with my idea, *fraud?*"

The smirk on Bixby's face said everything. After years of chasing Selvig, the man had finally shown up on his doorstep. The timing couldn't have been better. "Took you long enough," Bixby said. The crowd quieted. They were deeply engaged in the unfolding drama. "Jealous that I did what you couldn't? My Crescent is going to change the world. It made me nervous playing the long game, I'll admit. Courting you and that beautiful mind of yours was exhausting. I knew I drove you crazy, but I had to do it. Then I stopped. Wanna know why?" Bixby took joy in the slow burn of his revelations. "Girls used to crush on me all the time in high school. I'd chase them, they'd recoil. I'd stop chasing them, they'd come crawling to my doorstep. As a man of science and logic, you see where I'm going with this, yes? I knew once I stopped trying to court you, it was only a matter of time before you'd show up." Bixby leaned on the balcony railing, tilting his head ever so slightly. "Miss your motel? Never been to New Mexico myself, but

I *did* have an interesting conversation with a man named Ken who managed a little dive called the Sea-farer. Did you know Ken will do practically anything for money? *Some people*, right? No morals. Anyway, hope your room didn't have any *bug* problems."

That's how Bixby knew, Selvig thought.

Jane had moved into position while Bixby ranted. She peeked out from behind the balcony curtain and nodded to Selvig.

"Bixby, you're a disgrace to science! A manipulator who cares nothing for discovery or innovation. You're an egomaniac," Selvig declared. He looked around to rally the crowd and was met with a sea of blank stares. "Join with me, sisters and brothers! Together we will rise up and unseat this self-serving charlatan!"

The crowd was silent until a voice called out from the back of the room, "Selvig thinks he's better than us!"

Bixby's plan had worked better than he'd hoped. Selvig was in the lion's den, and it was about to be feeding time. An enormous flat-screen television descended from the ceiling. Bixby pressed a button on his watch and a video played. It was of Selvig running around Stonehenge naked while being chased by the police. The crowd roared with laughter. Selvig's stomach sank. He felt powerless and frustrated. Remembering the mission, he shook out of his funk and focused. Selvig made eye contact with Jane, who stealthily removed the Crescent from its suspiciously unguarded perch. The first phase of the plan was complete. Selvig scanned the room but couldn't find Darcy and Felix. Seconds ticked away as Jane reappeared at the foot of the stairs. She caught Bixby's eye, and everything went downhill.

"Stop that woman!" he shouted, rallying his followers. They weren't a particularly active bunch. Most of them avoided physical exercise. None had ever been in a fight. But their leader had given them a command and they loved to follow orders.

"Take that!" screeched a man wearing a name tag that read *Doctor Globulus*. He weakly tossed a nanite-filled Smart Blob at Jane. She dodged it with ease and took off toward the front door. Empowered by Globulus's act of bravery, the other attendees began grabbing nanite Blobs in an effort to stop Jane's exit. Selvig finally spotted Felix and Darcy. They were hovering near the Gene Drive booth.

"Time for the perfect, nonthreatening distraction. Killer bunnies, attack!" Felix shouted. He and Darcy swiftly tossed open each cage as the colony of rabbits quickly spread out across the floor. The crowd yelped and shrieked, tripping over themselves trying to avoid the bunnies.

Near the exit, a clunky, junky android had blocked Jane's escape. The midsize drone's body was made of dull metal and looked as if it had been cobbled together from a combination of old animatronic amusement park attractions and department store mannequins.

"What are you supposed to be?" Jane asked.

"I. AM. THE. VYSION," the robot belched. "YOU. WILL. GO. NO. FARTHER."

Undeterred, Jane reached into her waistband and retrieved a small, sharp blade. "Shoddy workmanship, inferior materials, and a general lack of imagination. Your *vision* is shortsighted. Now get out of my way!" She plunged the blade into the android's stomach, twisting as she ripped through the cheap metal, moving it all the way up through its head. Having been split in two, the android collapsed onto the ground in a pile of sparking circuits. "Shoulda been vibranium," Jane said, bolting to safety.

Selvig rushed to the exit, turning back to look at the chaos that had unfolded. On the balcony above, Bixby stared daggers. He was still, silent. The look on Bixby's face gave Selvig a sense of accomplishment.

"Go!" Darcy yelled, pushing Selvig out the door. "Reflect later!" The group ran down the driveway as fast as they could, out of breath as they reached the end.

"The cops are going to be here soon," Felix said.

"Where's your transportation, Erik?" asked Jane. The panicked look in Selvig's eyes answered her question. There was no transportation. *"Great."*

CHUCKA-CHUCKA-CHUCKA-CHUCKA-CHUCKA-CHUCKA.

A Tomahawk helicopter roared onto the scene, ominously hovering above.

Felix tried his best not to freak out. "We're *done*," he said, sweating. "I'm gonna end up in some kind of kid's prison where I have to fight my way through a preteen gang hierarchy, trading candy bars for potato chips, learning how to strangle people with my bare hands. All my dreams...my whole future...done!"

"Cool it, drama queen," Darcy said.

A rope ladder fell from the helicopter as a disembodied voice called out from inside. "C'mon! We don't have all day!"

Felix, Darcy, Jane, and Selvig were out of options. There was only one place to go, and that was *up*. They swiftly ascended into the helicopter to find Anjelica Tan, Anoki, and Bisi Banyaga waiting.

"Surprise!" Banyaga exclaimed gleefully. "Timing is everything."

Selvig was stunned, surprised, and incredibly thankful to be safe.

"Take a minute, catch your breath, and then we'll discuss business," Anoki said. "But also buckle up—we're going to Norway."

CHAPTER 10

"This is all happening so fast!" Felix shrieked.

Banyaga cackled from the pilot's seat, thoroughly entertained by Felix's outburst.

Anjelica Tan put her arm around Felix as if they were best buds. "We're going to the Water of Sight, kid," she said. "Hope you brought your swim trunks."

Darcy raised her hand. "Whose helicopter is this?"

Tan pointed at Anoki, who was hovering near Banyaga, helping guide the craft.

Darcy shook her head. "More of that sweet off-the-grid living, huh?"

"I'm not going to apologize for owning a helicopter," Anoki said. "Without it you'd all be running through the Hollywood Hills like insane people. Be grateful that Bisi, Anjelica, and I knew enough about Erik to put this plan in motion and save your collective rear ends."

"Foster!" Tan exclaimed. She grabbed Jane, looked her in the face, and gave her a tight squeeze. "I didn't want to say anything, but I knew you were out there somewhere, doing your thing." She leaned in close to Jane's ear, whispering covertly. "Erik was kind of a mess without you. Next time you leave town, give the guy a heads-up, huh?"

Anoki pointed to Jane's jacket. "You've got a spot of slime on your person," they said. "Please clean it off. I like to keep this vehicle spotless."

"Oh, sorry," Jane said, wiping away the goo.

Selvig sat in the corner of the craft, clutching the Crescent tightly, inspecting its bits with care and consideration. He was relieved to see his old friends, and grateful for the save, but he also feared what was in store for them once they reached their destination. Learning the existence of the Infinity Stones and their role in the universe was a game changer. While he experienced some level of comfort in knowing the truth, new questions arose. Dangerous uncertainties lay ahead. Accessing the Water of Sight was a great risk, but would it truly pay off? Selvig wasn't sure yet. Either way, there was definitely no turning back now.

Darcy sat down next to Selvig. "Can *we* get a helicopter?" she said, nudging his shoulder. "It's obvious we need one. *For science.*"

Selvig wasn't in the mood to talk. He was in his own head. His mind was consumed with the numerous scenarios they might face.

"We're doing this now, boss. The wheels are in motion," Darcy said. "Don't worry. Be happy?"

"Everyone out!" Banyaga shouted. He'd abruptly landed the helicopter at a private airstrip. "Grab your gear and get moving. Times a-wastin'."

Tan picked up two large duffel bags and swung them over her shoulder. "I assumed we'd need those Gravimetric Spikes of yours. I kept them in a cool, dry place. Should be in tip-top condition. Phase Meter is in here, too."

Felix lagged behind as the group exited the craft.

"*Ummmm*. I thought we were going to the Water of Sight."

"Boy, you can't fly a helicopter from California to Norway," Banyaga said. "We're taking *that*." He pointed to a sleek, black supersonic jet parked on the jetway. "All right, team, grab your gear and get on that plane. Norway awaits."

The team piled into the craft and settled into their seats.

"We'll need to fasten the Crescent to the Gravimetric Spikes," said Selvig. "The configuration will function as a conductor, absorbing the output of energy from the Water of Sight, refocusing it through the Spikes themselves, and ultimately opening an Einstein-Rosen bridge."

"No one told me to dress for space travel," Darcy said.

"If my theory is correct, this specific bridge won't allow for interstellar travel. Instead, it will become a galactic communication conduit," explained Selvig. "Make no mistake, the Water of Sight is an unknown quantity. Assigning it this kind of scientific context is difficult though not impossible. What we are embarking upon is dangerous. Untested. We must all be aware of the stakes."

"Theories get proven every single day," Banyaga said, leaning back in his chair. "I'm okay with getting sucked into a space portal if it means breaking some new ground. Science is sacrifice, right? Somebody write that down for me."

Jane carefully unveiled the Gravimetric Spikes. "These will need to be reconfigured a bit." She took them into her hands, looking them over closely. "I can make that happen, but I'll need some help."

Banyaga swung a heavy backpack onto the floor. It was overflowing with an array of unique tools. "These should serve your purpose," he said. "Be kind to my babies. Some are homemade. Handle them with the utmost care, and, please, use them wisely."

Felix pointed at the Crescent. "May I see? I promise not to break it." Selvig handed him the device. He looked it over, every nook and cranny. "The Water of Sight showed Thor visions, so we know it has the capacity to show *us* visions, too. I think I know how."

Jane handed him a Gravimetric Spike. "Let's see what you can do, kid."

As Felix got to work, Tan filled with nostalgia for past adventures. "This reminds me of the time—"

"*No.* Uh-uh, Anjelica Tan. This is *not* story time. This is *focus on the task at hand* time," Banyaga said. "I'm already exhausted."

"Silence!" shouted Anoki. "Let Jane and Felix do their work. This flight is shorter than you think. We'll arrive in Oslo, where a vehicle is waiting to transport us to Tønsberg as quickly as possible."

Tan leaned over to Darcy, speaking out of the side of her mouth. "Ian quit on me. Just thought you might want to know," she whispered. "I don't know what you said to him but *thank you.* Said he wasn't living up to his potential. Saved me the trouble of firing him. Wasn't the brightest bulb, that Ian. Sweet as pie, though."

Darcy was surprised by the unexpected news. "That's interesting."

"What about you?" Tan asked. "I get the sense you're kind of over this stuff."

"Good eye," Darcy said, exhaling. "After this is over, I think I might be out."

Tan leaned close to Darcy so no one else could hear. "I'm not about telling other people how to live their lives, but we both know you're too valuable to Erik's outfit to leave just yet. Believe me. The world is an increasingly dangerous place. It needs you."

"Don't start with the glue stuff again."

"Darcy, as a scientist you have a duty to uphold—"

"I'm not a scientist."

"Oh. Huh. Well, I don't know how I didn't know *that*, but it doesn't matter now. You're observant. You've picked up a few skills over the years. Obviously, you know how to manage egos and navigate tricky communications between unruly individuals. Take all that knowledge and put it to use in a new way. Reinvent yourself. I did. Think of this as the beginning of the rest of your life."

"At this moment in time, I'm going to concentrate on *not dying*."

Selvig sidled up to Banyaga, trying to play it cool but falling short. "Which one of you organized this rescue mission? How did you know we'd require your assistance?"

"I'm psychic," Banyaga deadpanned. "You wear your intentions on your sleeve, Erik. Anjelica, Anoki, and I saw this coming a mile away. You should be thankful we have a phone tree for these kinds of things. One calls the other and so on until we're all in a helicopter coming to save your butt. We're the Science Avengers now. Think of the uniforms and get on board!"

The Science Avengers. An idea like that usually made Selvig uncomfortable. However, this time, surrounded by his closest comrades, it didn't sound so unappealing.

Anoki lingered near Jane and Felix as they tinkered with the Gravimetric Spikes.

"Wanna help?" asked Felix. "Or are you just going to stand there judging my technique?"

"You're too young to have technique," Anoki replied. "I'm realizing that I miss these get-togethers more than I thought I would. Isolating oneself in nature can be great for clearing one's head...but it's also very boring."

"I understand the feeling," Jane said, adjusting the frequency of her Phase Meter. "It's good to be surrounded by friends."

The flight to Oslo was smooth, and the drive to Tøns-berg was quick. Anoki had planned their transportation down to a tee. The Water of Sight was located in a cavern outside the city's center in a secluded area that locals knew to avoid. The people of Tønsberg had learned their lessons. Hydra's theft of the Tesseract during the World War II invasion taught them that toying with powers they didn't understand simply wasn't worth the trouble. Selvig led his team through the forest on foot, arriving at the cavern in the middle of the night. They carefully filed into the subterranean space and surrounded the motionless pool. It was ordinary—lifeless—one might say. Selvig gazed deeply into the docile waters, mesmerized by the view.

"*Wake up*," commanded Anoki. "We didn't come all this way so you could stare at your little space bathtub all night. Chop-chop. There's work to do."

Jane set up the Gravimetric Spikes while Felix

adjusted the Crescent. He made doubly sure it was well fastened so as not to vibrate out of position during the event. Jane held her Phase Meter in the air, waving it around in all directions. "I'm not picking up any activity," she said. "It's like a dead zone, which is…odd."

"That device was sitting in storage for a while. Maybe it's out of juice?" suggested Tan.

Jane wasn't convinced. "It should work just fine. I upgraded it on the way here. Maybe this cave isn't the cosmic nexus it once was."

The group looked at one another and then at Selvig. No one was sure what to do next.

"Fire it up!" exclaimed Banyaga. "What's wrong with you people?"

The group positioned themselves behind a rocky column, safely away from the Water of Sight. The moment of truth had arrived. Selvig gave everyone a final warning before he flipped the switch. "There may be lightning. There may be static. We may tear through the fabric of reality. Be aware of your surroundings," he cautioned.

Felix was more than ready for action. *"Let's do this."* Using a remote control Jane had built in transit, he jolted each Spike with power, creating a gravity well above the pool. "And now for the final touch. This one's for you, Mom and Dad." He pressed the activation key, turning on the Crescent, which glowed bright white. The device released a low-pitched hum and was warm to the touch. Soon the air in the cave started vibrating. The Gravimetric Spikes shook uncontrollably. The apparatus was coming apart.

"Shut it down!" Selvig shouted.

Felix sheepishly ended the process as Jane assessed the damage. "The Spikes are too fragile."

"Just dial the whole thing down a notch," Darcy said. "See? I can do science, too."

"The Crescent is complex," Jane said. "Bisi, give it the Reverse Engineer once-over."

Banyaga took the Crescent into his hands, gently cracking it in half and assessing its insides. "There's a massive amount of energy channeling through this thing. The Spikes can't process it efficiently.

That's why everything is breaking apart. We need to absorb the output."

Felix reached into his pocket and produced the Kimoyo Bead he'd swiped from Anjelica's bunker. "This should do the trick," he said, showing off the small but powerful item. "At least, I *think* it should."

"Hey!" Tan exclaimed.

Felix was deeply embarrassed. "I didn't mean to steal it from you, I swear! It kind of just happened. Can I keep it, though?"

"Beg *later*," Banyaga said, pointing at the Crescent.

Felix carefully shimmied the bead into the device, then reattached it to the Spike. "We're good to go. The heat should dial down to a manageable level." Despite having solved the issue, there was a sadness in Felix's eyes.

"Look alive," nudged Banyaga. "You may have saved the day."

"Yeah, but…" Felix struggled to communicate what was really on his mind. "I lost the coolest thing I've ever owned in my entire life. Like, when am I ever going to get another piece of Wakanda? I mean a *real* piece of Wakanda. Life isn't fair, man."

"Of course not. Life can be terrible! But let me tell you something, young man, there's a future for you in this world," Banyaga explained. "When all of this is over (which I hope is soon) we're going to have a conversation. I'll *upgrade* that bead, okay? Trust in Bisi."

"That's *my* Kimoyo Bead you're talking about," Tan protested. *"Stolen property."*

"Stand back!" Selvig shouted. He pushed everyone away from the water's edge as the team returned to their safe space. Felix activated the Crescent and the Gravimetric Spikes shook once more. Gusts of powerful wind swept through the cavern, stirring up dust and rock. Electricity danced across the Water of Sight, flickering like fireflies. The Spikes shook harder and harder. For a moment it looked as if they'd collapse completely until—

BOOM!

KRACK-A-THOOM!

Suddenly, the chaos stopped. An eerie hum filled

the cavern as the apparatus buzzed with electro-magnetism. Above the Water of Sight, on the cavern ceiling, a wormhole slowly opened up and spread itself out across the space like a grand tapestry. Unlike a typical Einstein-Rosen bridge, this gateway wasn't meant for traveling. It was a window into the unknown. The galaxy had opened up to reveal its insides. Brilliant stars pulsed across a pitch-black sky. It was the birth of existence. The dawn of the cosmos. The assembled team struggled to make sense of the chaotic beauty. Planets formed, before exploding into stardust. Six bold flashes of color appeared: red, blue, purple, green, yellow, and orange. The Infinity Stones blinked like holiday lights across a map of the stars. Its story unfolded like a silent movie.

The Space Stone, too powerful for its own good, bounced from place to place until it settled into its containment vessel, giving birth to the Tesseract. The glowing blue cube changed hands through the centuries, traveling to Earth, falling into the hands of the Red Skull, becoming a pawn used by Loki, and eventually ending up in the possession of a mysterious purple-hued Titan. Though the assembled team was unaware of his identity, the universe knew him well. *Thanos.* In an instant, he disappeared, replaced by the bloodred glow of the Reality Stone. Once in the possession of Malekith and the Dark Elves, the mass of energy known as the Aether reached its creeping tentacles across the galaxy. As one of its host bodies, Doctor Foster saw herself depicted in the assortment of images, if only for a brief moment. She was now part of cosmic history, whether she liked it or not. Next, a white-haired eccentric was shown begging for his life. The Collector, once the proud inheritor of the Reality Stone, had his prize taken from him by Thanos, who'd now become a recurring presence in universal history. Selvig made a mental note. Thanos's face was one he vowed not to forget. Soon the cavern went dark, filling with a thin coating of mist. The Infinity Gauntlet emerged from within a cloud of smoke, reaching out for something to hold on to, but, instead, finding nothing. Frustrated, the golden glove snapped its fingers as beings across a thousand worlds turned to ash. Heroes, villains, alien beings from undiscovered worlds. Faces that were both familiar and strange. Heartbreaking images of pain and suffering blinked in and out like an old film strip. The sight was almost too much to bear. The dusty remains of the dead soon swirled into a cyclone that grew smaller and smaller until it twisted itself into a tiny amber pebble. It hung quivering in the air above the Water of Sight, coating the room in a warm orange light. The Soul Stone radiated a surprising sense of wholeness. Despite all they'd witnessed, the assembled group felt at ease. It was as if, at last, everything were going to be all right.

Hurried footsteps rushed through the cavern's entrance, crushing pebbles as they stomped. Ignatius Bixby was *angry*. "You don't deserve this!" He swung a thick steel rod through the air, smashing the Gravimetric Spikes over and over again until they were damaged beyond repair. The portal quickly evaporated, and the images dissolved as if they'd never even appeared. The story of the Infinity Stones ended abruptly, never to return. Bixby made sure of that. He ripped the Crescent from its connection. "Stay! Away!" he screamed, wildly swinging the steel rod. "I invited all of you to my table and this is how you repay me?" He was out of breath and panting like a dog. "I assumed petty theft was beneath you, Erik, but I'm glad you played your hand just as I expected you would. Didn't exactly expect it all to go down like this, but what do I know, anyway? I'm just some dummy who wants to be on TV, right?" He clutched the Crescent and held it close. "I had this baby built fairly quickly. Turned out nice, don't you think? Erik's concept. My execution. Match made in hell." Bixby smashed the Gravimetric Spikes a final time. "I certainly don't need *those* worthless things." He opened a compartment on the underside of the Crescent and pressed a series of buttons. The device purred. "Fail-safe! Didn't think of that, did you? Now I'm good to go."

"Ignatius, you must understand something," Selvig said. His tone was careful and considered. He didn't want to escalate the situation. "The Water of Sight is an overwhelming cosmic force. A human being simply cannot step—"

"I know what it is, Erik!" Bixby yelled. "You led me right to it. Anoki isn't the only rich kid with a jet." The Crescent's purr grew louder. "I'm protected. You have no idea." He pointed at Selvig and winked. "Catch you on the flip side, suckers!" Bixby plunged himself into the Water of Sight, which erupted in a web of electricity. Deafening thunderclaps echoed through the cavern. Bixby's body was sucked up out of the pool and into the storm of heat and light. His eyes bulged. His body shook. Raw cosmic power coursed through his body, and then it spat him out against the cavern wall. The unforgiving Water of Sight swallowed the Crescent completely before returning to its natural state. The once-boiling liquid was calm anew. The group surrounded Bixby's body as it lay motionless on the ground.

"*I'm* not touching him," Felix said.

Jane knelt down and took Bixby's pulse. "He's

alive. His vital signs are surprisingly regular, but we need to get him to a doctor."

"Um, I need to ask you guys something," Darcy said sheepishly. "We just witnessed a lot of crazy stuff in that cosmic cloud thingy, but did you also see a *tree person* and a *raccoon with a gun* at one point?"

"Yes," the group answered in unison.

"Cool, cool. Just checking."

Selvig stood at the edge of the water, struggling to comprehend everything he'd just witnessed. Though Bixby's appearance and sudden collapse were unexpected turns of events, prior to that an amazing thing had happened. After years of theories, questions, and endless wondering, Erik Selvig finally had *answers*. They were beautiful, confusing, and incomplete. It would take time to piece them all together. New resources needed to be tapped. There would be discussion, inquiry, and a collision of ideas. The Infinity Stones were to be fully investigated. Selvig felt energized. A new mystery had taken shape, and he was ready to seek the truth. He looked around the cavern and felt at peace. He was surrounded by friends. People who stood by his side despite his flaws. He quietly vowed never to take them for granted again.

"Are we finished?" Anoki asked, arms folded. "I don't mean to be insensitive, but keeping a jet fueled and ready for takeoff at a moment's notice is costly."

"Cheapskate," murmured Banyaga.

"Oh! Hey!" Darcy exclaimed. She pulled out the bag of test tube key chains she'd gotten at the Dollar Holler and passed them out to the assembled team. "For a job well done."

"Question *everything*. Learn *something*. Answer *nothing*," Tan said. She put her arm around Selvig's shoulders and squeezed. "Euripides said that, not me."

Felix tapped Selvig on the shoulder. "What's on your mind, Doc?"

Selvig grinned. "The future."

One Month Later

Selvig had been standing outside the large, rusty metal dome for the past fifteen minutes. Once used as a military facility, it sat vacant on the outskirts of Puente Antiguo for years until Anjelica Tan snatched it up at a discount for reasons that still remained murky. Selvig circled the structure, waiting for his tardy lunch companion to appear. The heat was causing him to sweat more than usual, though—surprisingly—he didn't find the discomfort annoying.

After the incident at the Water of Sight and the revelation of the Infinity Stones, Selvig took a step back to reorganize his life and work. Solving the greatest mystery mankind had ever faced required immense focus. Now Selvig could see things clearly and was taking the proper steps to make sure his mind remained sharp. Though he hadn't anticipated a return to Puente Antiguo, Selvig had also learned to expect the unexpected.

"*YOOOOOOOOO!*" a voice screamed from above. "What's up, Doc?"

Selvig looked up to find Felix hovering in the air, wearing a pair of homemade gravity boots.

"How ya like me now?" Felix said.

"Bisi told me you were in your element here, tinkering with his devices and such."

Felix rolled his eyes. "Understatement of the century." He adjusted the controls and powered down his boots, landing safely on the pavement. "Made my 'skywalkers' the first day. They're a little wonky on the takeoff, but I'm working on it. There's so much I can do with all Doctor Banyaga's junk." He carefully glanced over each shoulder. "I'm not supposed to call it that, but whatever. Next up I want to design something totally crazy, like cybernetic rhino armor. This old place can be super boring some days, but having access to all kinds of tools and materials to build with is straight *fire*."

"I'm pleased to see you're adjusting to your new circumstances with vim and vigor."

"What's up with Bixby?" Felix asked. "Saw a story online about him 'hitting his head while on an expedition to uncover the secrets of the universe.' His dummy fans think he's a hero now. I almost vomited all over my computer."

"Ignatius is in a coma at the moment, being well cared for by a team of trusted doctors. He's expected to make a full recovery."

"Hope he rots—"

"Human beings can be selfish, cruel, and violent. They can also be rehabilitated. It's my sincere hope that when Ignatius wakes, he chooses the latter. Only time will tell."

"Don't bet on it. The dude is slime."

In the distance, a shiny silver sports car approached, recklessly swerving through the open desert, leaving a cloud of dirt and dust to swirl in its wake.

"A lot of joyriders out here in the middle of nowhere," Felix said. "Stupid *kids*."

Selvig stifled a chuckle as the car loudly screeched to a stop. Its door flung open. Darcy stepped out wearing a tasteful black dress with a short gray sport coat, brand-new designer sunglasses, and a bright smile.

"You're late," Selvig scolded.

"Let me have a dramatic entrance, old man," said Darcy. "You owe me."

Felix circled the sparkling vehicle in awe, checking out every detail. "Nice *whip*! There's definitely no way you could ever in a million years afford this on what you make."

"It's a rental," replied Darcy. "Erik still needs to buy me a new car."

"Ah yes," Selvig said. "I keep forgetting about that."

Felix eyed Darcy suspiciously. "You're dressed for either *court* or *church*."

"*Awww*. This ol' thing?" Darcy said, giving a playful twirl.

"Which is it? If it's court, can I come and watch you get sentenced? I promise I'll be quiet as long as I can come visit you in jail. If it's church? Hard pass."

"I *almost* missed you, Felix," replied Darcy. "Unfortunately, I need to bail on lunch. A work thing suddenly sprang up, and I've got to turn around and go back to the airport."

"*But you just got here*," Felix whined. "I haven't even shown you my workshop!"

"Relax. I know what a teenage boy's bedroom is like," said Darcy. "I'm sure *yours* is fairly disgusting."

"Darcy has taken on an enhanced role in our outfit," Selvig said. "One that utilizes her skill set to the fullest."

"And takes up every ounce of my free time. Go figure. But I'd be lying if I said it didn't feel good. My working title is Head of Science-Based Initiatives, which is a fancy way of saying I'll be asking people for money to fund important research projects. Not only that, but I'm also designing science-based programs for schools and communities in need. I'm heading to Washington, DC, to meet with Senator Harrison about making these programs a reality."

"From *basic* to *boss*," Felix said. "I like it."

"Just putting my major to good use. *Finally*," she said. "The bad news is most of Harrison's political campaigns have been funded by science deniers. He's not the kind of legislator who respects what we do. Unfortunately, he also heads a committee that decides who gets the money, so I have no choice but to deal with him. I'm putting my best foot forward and keeping my fingers crossed he sees things our way."

"Senator Harrison is an idiot," Felix growled. "That guy thinks the earth is flat!"

"Don't worry, I'm bringing along a packet of, let's call it, *opposition research*. If he gives me a hard time, I'll just politely show him the photographs I acquired of him on the beach smooching a red-haired woman who is not his wife and hope it changes his mind."

"Darcy, we agreed. No blackmailing," Selvig warned. "We fight our fight with merit."

"Chill out, Erik. I've also got stacks of data on the benefits of embracing scientific pursuit. Science isn't just about Super Hero craziness and new technology. It's about enhancing people's ability to solve practical problems and make informed decisions. If Harrison says no, he'll *literally* be saying no to the future. If he does *that*, then, well, you'd best believe I'll make him regret it for the rest of his life."

"*Ooooo*, she likes to get her hands dirty," Felix said. "I'm impressed."

"And what *I* am is a *professional*," Darcy said. "A professional who needs to get going."

A hatch atop the dome flung open. Bisi Banyaga's head poked out. "Erik, I *know* you're not here distracting my student when he's got *things to do*."

"Oh yeah. So. I kind of can't do lunch, either," admitted Felix. "I'm really behind on an experiment and need the time to work. Doctor Banyaga will kill me if I miss another project deadline."

"Felix..." Selvig began.

"I know, I know, I know."

"We've discussed this...."

"Doc…"

"If you plan on attending the Wakandan Outreach Centre.…"

"I need to raise my game!" Felix shouted. "Got it! Thank you! Heard it before! Will you please get off my back?!" Obviously embarrassed by his outburst, Felix recalibrated. "Sorry. The heat has me shook."

"Mmhmm. Blame *the heat* for your slacking," Banyaga said, shaking his head. "We're all melting, boy. Handle your business."

"How goes it, Bisi?" Selvig asked. "Enjoying your new accommodations?"

Banyaga cackled wildly. "You've got a lot of nerve asking me that question, Erik Selvig. A *lot* of nerve."

"He's still unpacking. Oh, and the toilets in this place aren't exactly functional," Felix whispered. "We're still working out the kinks."

"*I can hear you!*" Bisi shouted. "The toilets are just fine. When I'm done upgrading them they'll be top-of-the-line sanitational experiences. Believe it."

"Your resources will increase soon enough, old

friend," assured Selvig. "Our grand plan is taking shape. Give it time."

"Ticktock, Erik," Banyaga said. *"Tick. Tock."* He descended into the depths and slammed down the hatch.

"Well, I suppose I'll just have to enjoy a nice cheeseburger on my own, then." Selvig shrugged.

"What's this *grand plan* of yours, and do the other Science Avengers know about it?" Felix asked. He clearly knew the name would get a rise out of Selvig.

"I'd prefer you not use that moniker to describe our gathering of minds," Selvig said, avoiding the question.

"Anoki says hello. They're back in school finishing their degree," Darcy replied. "They've also graciously donated a big chunk of change to build our new—"

"We needn't go into those details, Darcy," Selvig said, cutting her off. "Doctor Foster sends her regrets. She wanted to be here but her work—"

"Took precedence. I know," Felix said. His voice quieted. "I've been thinking about the Infinity

Stones. The patterns and possibilities. I've got a new theory that might blow this whole thing wide open. Tell Doctor Foster I'm emailing her. You want me to copy you?"

"I'd be honored."

"Seriously though, Doc. What's this dome all about? Talk," Felix pressed. "I'm a part of this team now so throw me a bone. I've earned it. You know, I thought after our mission ended, you were gonna chill out for a while, but I know you're planning something. *What?*"

Selvig smiled. "*Expansion*, Felix. That's what's required now more than ever. Like the universe in its infancy, a scientist's work must grow and keep growing. We mustn't give up. Not when there are so many new mysteries to solve and battles to fight. The odds may be stacked against us, but that's why we'll surround ourselves with individuals who inspire our work and keep us in check. I'd forgotten that for a time." He looked up to the sky and took a long, deep breath. "The end is never really the end, is it? There's always more to be done."

ACKNOWLEDGMENTS

Writing the Cosmic Quest series filled me with a huge amount of joy (and stress!). I'm grateful Mary-Kate Gaudet helped me keep it together. She's a supportive, encouraging editor who values creativity. Who could ask for anything more? My favorite part of the process was when she'd text me lines that made her laugh. Russ Busse, meanwhile, is an unstoppable force of positive energy who will rule this world one day. Just you watch. Regan Winter? She's totally on top of it. As the MCU's secret weapon, Will Corona Pilgrim really knows his stuff. His guidance and knowledge were invaluable resources. There's lots of science in *The Cosmic Quest: Volume Two: Aftermath*, and it came together because of Amy Brown and the Science & Entertainment Exchange. They're an amazing organization everyone should check out. Thank you to James Kakalios, Nureddin Ashammakhi, and Frank Macabenta, for providing me with official science-y talk that I'm still trying to understand. Thank you as well to Sandra Cohen, Siena Koncsol, Amanda Marquez, and Stefanie Hoffman at Little, Brown; Elana Cohen at Marvel Press; Eleena Khamedoost and Ariel Gonzalez at Marvel Studios; and Mary-Ann Zissimos and Cindy Malouf at Disney Publishing. Travis Kramer, your patience is legendary. Terry and Jean Snider, thank you for birthing me. Jeff Goldblum, can you get in touch, please?

ABOUT THE AUTHOR

BRANDON T. SNIDER has authored over one hundred books featuring a host of pop culture favorites, but he'd give it all up to write the Collector's and Grandmaster's adventures for the rest of his days. Brandon lives in New York City, where he's a member of the Writers Guild of America. Visit him online at cootiekid.com.